"A five course meal: loaded with pleasure . . . but offering enough protein and complex carbohydrates to satisfy both body and soul. . . . Bank mixes humor with sadness while leavening difficulty with laughter to create a rich narrative that gratifies on many levels."
—*Los Angeles Times*

"Bank's bittersweet, tremendously winning return [is] . . . enthralling and engaging."
—Jennifer Weiner, *Entertainment Weekly*

"The legion of fans of Bank's bestselling first book, a collection of linked stories called *The Girl's Guide to Hunting and Fishing*, will recognize in her novel a brutally astute and accurate way of writing about love. . . . Truly compelling and . . . eminently readable."
—*Chicago Tribune*

"Marvelous . . . Bank's sharp wit and streamlined prose serve Sophie's exquisitely honed female sensibility, placing the author squarely in the tradition of Clare Boothe Luce and Nora Ephron. Like them, Bank possesses a prodigious talent for snappy one-liners, and her self-deprecating anecdotes belie intelligence and sophistication. In short, [it] purrs."
—*The Washington Post*

"Prodigiously talented, mordantly wry and wise, Bank offers . . . irresistible reading."
—*San Francisco Chronicle*

"Elegantly funny . . . Forget sophomore slump: this book proves that the second time's a charm. In Bank's case, it's equal parts brains and charm. . . . Bank works her magic . . . Vital and fresh and funny."
—*Chicago Sun-Times*

"Six years ago [Melissa Bank] was prematurely said to have written a wise, ingratiating set of stories about a smart young woman and her fractious Jewish family. Now she has actually done it. . . . Ms. Bank brings a funny, jaundiced viewpoint."
—Janet Maslin, *The New York Times*

"Bank's casual writing style and snappy dialogue make Sophie's misadventures in womanhood both funny and emotionally resonant."
—*People*

"[An] engaging, lightly ironic, loose-limbed portrait of a contemporary young woman adrift in the sea of New York City. . . . Bank has done it again."
—*St. Louis Post-Dispatch*

PENGUIN BOOKS

THE WONDER SPOT

Melissa Bank is the author of *The Girls' Guide to Hunting and Fishing*. A winner of the Nelson Algren Award for Short Fiction, she divides her time between New York City and East Hampton, New York.

To request Penguin Readers Guides by mail
(while supplies last), please call (800) 778-6425
or e-mail reading@us.penguingroup.com.
To access Penguin Readers Guides online, visit our
Web site at www.penguin.com.

THE WONDER SPOT

MELISSA BANK

PENGUIN BOOKS

PENGUIN BOOKS
Published by the Penguin Group
Penguin Group (USA) Inc., 375 Hudson Street, New York, New York 10014, U.S.A.
Penguin Group (Canada), 90 Eglinton Avenue East, Suite 700, Toronto,
Ontario, Canada M4P 2Y3 (a division of Pearson Penguin Canada Inc.)
Penguin Books Ltd, 80 Strand, London WC2R 0RL, England
Penguin Ireland, 25 St Stephen's Green, Dublin 2, Ireland (a division of Penguin Books Ltd)
Penguin Group (Australia), 250 Camberwell Road, Camberwell,
Victoria 3124, Australia (a division of Pearson Australia Group Pty Ltd)
Penguin Books India Pvt Ltd, 11 Community Centre,
Panchsheel Park, New Delhi - 110 017, India
Penguin Group (NZ), cnr Airborne and Rosedale Roads, Albany,
Auckland 1310, New Zealand (a division of Pearson New Zealand Ltd)
Penguin Books (South Africa) (Pty) Ltd, 24 Sturdee Avenue,
Rosebank, Johannesburg 2196, South Africa

Penguin Books Ltd, Registered Offices: 80 Strand, London WC2R 0RL, England

First published in the United States of America by Viking Penguin,
a member of Penguin Group (USA) Inc. 2005
Published in Penguin Books 2006

1 3 5 7 9 10 8 6 4 2

The story "The Wonder Spot," appeared in different form in *Speaking with the Angel,*
edited by Nick Hornby, Riverhead Books, 2001.

Grateful acknowledgment is made for permission to reprint excerpts from the following copyrighted
works: "Highway 61 Revisited" by Bob Dylan. Copyright © 1965 by Warner Bros. Inc. Copyright ©
renewed 1993 by Special Rider Music. All rights reserved. International copyright secured. Reprinted
by permission. "Shake and shake the ketchup bottle" by Richard Armour. By permission of the Estate
of Richard Armour. "Another Reason Why I Don't Keep a Gun in the House" and "The Rival Poet"
from *The Apple That Astonished Paris* by Billy Collins. Copyright © 1988 by Billy Collins. Reprinted
with permission of the University of Arkansas Press.

THE LIBRARY OF CONGRESS HAS CATALOGED THE HARDCOVER EDITION AS FOLLOWS:
Bank, Melissa.
The wonder spot / Melissa Bank.
p. cm.
ISBN 0-670-03411-8 (hc.)
ISBN 0 14 30.3721 8 (pbk.)
1. Jewish families—Fiction.   2. Teenage girls—Fiction.
3. Jewish women—Fiction.   4. Young women—Fiction.   I. Title
PS3552.A487 W66 2005
813'.52—dc22   2004061189

Printed in the United States of America
Set in Adobe Garamond

For my sister, Margery Bates

CONTENTS

BOSS OF THE WORLD

You COULD TELL it was going to be a perfect beach day, maybe the best one all summer, maybe the last one of our vacation, and we were going to spend it at my cousin's bat mitzvah in Chappaqua, New York. My mother had weeks ago gone over exactly what my brothers and I would wear; now, suddenly, she worried that my dress, bought particularly for this event, wasn't dressed-up enough. She despaired at the light cotton, no longer seeing the tiny, hand-embroidered blue flowers she'd been so charmed by in the store. She said the dress looked "peasanty," which was what I liked about it. Maybe tights would help, she said; did I have tights? "No," I said, and my face added, *Why would I bring tights to the seashore?* When she said that we could pick some up on the way to Chappaqua, I reminded her that the only shoes I had with me were the sandals I had on. I said, "They'll look great with tights."

"You don't have any other shoes?"

"Flip-flops," I said. "Sneakers."

My older brother came to my door. "Dad says we have to go."

She turned to Jack now and said, "Is your jacket small?"

If it was, I didn't see it, but my mother had already worked herself up into what she called a tizzy. "How is it possible for a person to outgrow a suit in a matter of weeks?" she wondered aloud, as though we had an unsolvable mystery or a miracle before us, instead of the result of Jack lifting weights and running all summer. He'd lost his blubber and added muscles where once there had been none; about once a day I'd put my hand around his bicep, and he'd flex it for me.

My father appeared in my doorway. "Just unbutton the jacket," he said.

Jack did, and my mother said a small, "Oh."

Then my father said, "Let's go," meaning, *We are going now.*

We followed our leader out to the driveway.

My little brother, Robert, was already in the station wagon, reading *All About Bats*, in his irreproachable seersucker suit. Beside him, our standard poodle sat tall and regal, facing the windshield as though anticipating the scenery to come.

When my mother tried to coax the dog out of the car, Robert said, "He wants to come with us."

"The dog will be more comfortable here," she said.

I thought, *We'd all be more comfortable here.*

Robert said, "Please don't call Albert 'the dog.' "

My father said, "Never mind, Joyce," and my mother said, "Fine," in the tone of, *I give up.*

I was about to get in the car when she said, "You're not wearing a slip." I'd decided slips were a pointless formality, like the white gloves my mother had finally given up asking me to wear. But she said, "You can see right through."

I was horrified: All I had on were white underpants. "You can?"

Robert said, "Just in the sun," and I relaxed; bat mitzvahs were seldom held alfresco.

My father said, "Everybody in the car."

I sat in the way back of the station wagon with Albert, farthest from my mother's tizzy and my father's irritation, though I would also be farthest from the air-conditioning, which would be turned on once my mother realized the wind was messing up her hair.

Until then, my brothers rolled their windows down, and Albert and I caught what breeze we could.

I had to close my eyes when we drove by the parking lot for the beach, but Robert turned full around at the tennis courts.

"Dad?" he said. "If we get home early enough, will you hit with me?"

I could hear the effort it took for my father to make his voice gentle: "We won't get home early enough."

Robert said, "But if we do?"

"If we do," my father said, "I would be delighted to hit with you."

Robert was just going into fifth grade and would probably be the smallest boy in his class again, but he was almost as good a tennis player as my father. Robert ran for every shot, no matter how hopelessly high or unhittably hard; he was as consistent as a backboard. At the courts, he'd play with anyone who asked—the lacquered ladies who needed a fourth, the stubby surgeon who kept a lit cigarette gritted between his teeth, the little girl who got distracted by butterflies.

· · · · ·

On the Garden State Parkway, nobody spoke. My parents were miserable, probably because they'd agreed not to smoke in the car. Robert was miserable because they were, though he was the reason they weren't smoking. He was always begging them to quit, and they half pretended they had.

I was miserable because we were rushing toward the boredom only a bat mitzvah could bring.

Jack seemed oblivious; he was looking out the window. Maybe he was imagining himself away at college, which he and my father talked about nonstop. Whenever I reminded Jack that it was a whole year away, he'd say how fast it would go; I'd say, "How do you know?" a question apparently undeserving of a reply.

· · · · ·

Rebecca, whose bat mitzvah we were going to celebrate, was hardly even related to me. Our mothers were distant cousins who'd learned to walk on the same street of row houses in West Philadelphia, and then when their families had moved to the suburbs, the cousins had gone to the same private school, camp, and college. I'd seen pictures of them as babies in sun bonnets in Atlantic City, as girls in plaid shorts in the Adirondacks, as young women in sunglasses in Paris. Both were petite, both had dark hair, and my mother said that both had gotten too thin during their phase of Jackie Onassis worship.

In my opinion, Aunt Nora was still too thin, and Rebecca was even thinner. She was a ballerina and kept her shoulders back too far and her head up too high; she would sometimes swoop into ballet jumps out of nowhere—when the four of us were trying to find the car in a parking lot, for example.

That winter she'd been the understudy for Clara in *The Nutcracker Suite* in New York City, and my mother had insisted we go. I said, "In case the real Clara breaks her leg?"

"We're going because it'll be fun," she said. "It's an enormous honor for Rebecca to be in the ballet."

"She's not in it," I said.

During the ballet I tried to be open-minded, but it made no sense to me; it seemed as likely for a girl to dance with a nutcracker as with a corkscrew or an egg beater.

During lunch, when Aunt Nora asked how I'd liked the performance, I said, "It wasn't my cup of tea," a phrase my mother had instructed me to use in place of *yuck* but which now seemed to affect Aunt Nora as my *yuck*s had my mother.

Flustered, I told Rebecca that I was sure the ballet would have been better if she'd been in it, and added a sympathetic, "I'm sorry you weren't picked."

I didn't realize my mistake until Rebecca scowled. Aunt Nora gave my mother a look, which was the same as talking about me while I was there.

On the train back to Philadelphia, my mother pretended that the four of us had enjoyed a splendid afternoon. She admired how thin and delicate Rebecca was. "Like a long-stemmed rose," she said.

I said, "She's more like a long piece of hair with hair."

I expected my mother to be angry, but instead she seemed almost glad—not that she said so. What she said was, "You might become friends when you're older."

I said, "I don't think so."

"Why not, puss?"

I shrugged. I told her that Rebecca had turned down a piece of gum I'd offered by saying, "I don't chew gum—it's not ladylike."

My mother saw nothing wrong with this; it was something she herself might've said. She repeated a ditty from her early life with

Aunt Nora: "We don't smoke and we don't chew, and we don't go with boys who do."

My mother told the same stories over and over—maybe twenty-five in all; if you added them up, there were only about two hours of her life that she wanted me to know about.

·　·　·　·　·

At a rest stop on the New Jersey Turnpike, we stretched our legs until my mother returned from the ladies' room.

When she did, Robert said, "You look great, Mom."

She did look great. The day before, she'd driven herself to Philadelphia to have her hair professionally colored, a wise decision, as her hair had turned orangey in the sun.

Back in the car, my father said he liked her dress, a mod print in yellow and pink.

I said, "It's a designer dress," which was what my mother had told me.

Now that the trouble seemed to have passed and the air-conditioning was on, I considered asking Robert to trade places with me.

My father, who could be what my mother called a reverse snob, said that all dresses were designer dresses; someone had designed them.

"Not Pucci," my mother said in a haughty voice.

"Ah," my father said, "putting on the dog," which was supposed to be a joke, but she didn't laugh.

I stayed where I was. I patted Albert's fleecy black coat. Looking into his sad eyes, I said, "I know just how you feel."

·　·　·　·　·

We were on the exit ramp for Chappaqua when my mother turned around and smiled in a way that had nothing to do with happiness. It was her way of saying, *Smile*, without risking the opposite, at least from me.

Before we walked into the synagogue, she said, "I'm so proud of all of you," like she was making a commercial about our family.

This synagogue was about twice as big as the one we went to, and

the service seemed ten times as long, as it was almost entirely in Hebrew, a language I did not speak.

Finally Rebecca went to the podium, her toes pointed out. She
seemed glad to be up there, in her chiffony pink dress, white tights,
and black Mary Janes. She wore her hair back in a looped braid tied
with a pink satin ribbon, though she might as well have been wearing
a halo the way my mother gazed up at her.

For a second Rebecca looked out at the audience, at her family and
her friends and her family's friends and all of the religious fanatics
who had chosen to spend the most beautiful day of the entire summer
inside. It occurred to me that she saw us as her public, and maybe she
wished she could dance the part of Clara that she'd worked so hard to
learn.

Then she looked down at the Torah the rabbi had ceremoniously
undressed and unscrolled, and she began to read aloud. I kept thinking that she would have to stop soon, but I was wrong about that. She
seemed to be reading the entire Torah up there.

Maybe she'd learned how to pronounce the Hebrew words, but
you could tell she had no idea what they meant. She read with zero
expression, as though reciting the Hebrew translation of a phone book
or soup label, the only semblance of an intonation a pause at the end
of a listing or ingredient.

In contrast, my mother, who was no more fluent in Hebrew than
I, appeared utterly enthralled; she even nodded occasionally as though
finding this or that passage especially insightful and moving.

Hebrew comprehension wasn't the only thing my mother was faking. When I pulled her wrist over to look at her watch and made a
face that signified, *I'm dying,* she posed her mouth in a smile. Then
she held my hand as though we were in love.

I couldn't see my father, but I thought he probably liked how long
the service was. He'd become more religious since his own father had
died. Before, my father had only gone to services on the major holidays with us, but now he sometimes went on Friday nights, too. He
walked, as the Orthodox did, even though he was heading toward our

Reform synagogue, the least religious one possible. Usually my mother went with him, but one night he'd gone alone. I'd watched him from my window, and it was strange to see him walking down our suburban street by himself.

. . . . .

I was so relieved when the service was over that I let my mother kiss me. Then it was time to go downstairs to what was called a luncheon instead of lunch.

The catering hall was decorated with pink curtains, pink carpeting, and pink tablecloths; a pink tutu encircled each centerpiece of pink roses. Even the air seemed pink.

My mother found the pink place card with my name and table number; she announced that I was sitting with Rebecca and the other twelve- and thirteen-year-olds at table #13, as in, *Great news!* Like most adults, my mother seemed to believe that a nearby birth date was all kids required for instant friendship.

I told her that I hoped she got to sit with the other forty-one- and forty-two-year-olds.

I spotted #13 at the edge of the dance floor but took my time getting there; I circled tables, pretending I didn't know where mine was. When I did sit down, Rebecca didn't even look up; I imagined her saying to her mother, *Does Sophie have to sit with us?*

The boy next to her resembled the boy I liked at my school, Eric Green—blond, dimples—and he must have asked who I was; I heard Rebecca say the words *My cousin,* while her tone said, *Nobody.*

The bandleader called Rebecca's grandparents up to the stage to say the blessing over the candles; he said, "Put your hands together for Grandpa Nathan," while the band played "Light My Fire."

I felt free to eat my roll.

Then a girl wearing a gold necklace that spelled *Alyssa* in script said, "Where are you from?"

"Surrey, Pennsylvania," I said. "It's outside of Philadelphia."

"I've been to the Pennsylvania Dutch country," she said. "You know, the Amish?"

I'd been there, too, and was about to say so, but she turned away from me, as though living in Pennsylvania instead of New York made me less like her than the somber people whose beliefs forbade the driving of cars and the wearing of zippers.

To the table at large, Alyssa said, "Who's going to Lori's bat mitzvah?"

I felt a pang that I hadn't been invited to the bat mitzvah of a girl I didn't even know.

I was wishing I could get up and leave, but a second later there was no need; the band went from "Hava Nagila" to "Jeremiah Was a Bull-frog," and everybody at my table got up to dance. I saw that all the girls were wearing tights; they probably had slips on, too.

I ate my chicken and watched the dance floor.

You could tell Rebecca saw herself as the belle of the bat mitzvah, but the grace that served her so well in ballet deserted her at rock 'n' roll. Maybe she wasn't used to dancing with her heels on the ground; she marched like a majorette in a parade or, it occurred to me, like the nutcracker in *The Nutcracker*.

The boy who looked like Eric Green danced like him, too; he barely did anything except jerk his overgrown bangs out of his eyes and mouth the occasional phrase, such as, "Joy to the fishes in the deep blue sea."

He stayed in one spot while Alyssa go-go danced around him. I studied her, trying to memorize the way she shimmied and swiveled; then I remembered that I'd tried moves like these in front of the mirror in my parents' bedroom and discovered the huge gap between how I wanted to look when I danced and how I actually did look.

I got up to visit my brothers. But Robert was performing his disappearing-nickel trick for the children's table, and Jack was sitting between two girls. One with wavy hair and glasses was making him laugh, and the other, very pretty, was jiggling one high heel to the music. I wished that for once he would like the funny one, but as I stood there I saw him ask the other girl to dance.

I almost bumped into Aunt Nora greeting guests at the eighty-plus table. She wore a pale blue sleeveless dress and her hair up in a bun plus bangs. It seemed possible that she was trying to look like Audrey Hepburn, and she did a little; both gave the impression of fragility, though Aunt Nora's seemed to come from tension and Audrey's from innocence.

Aunt Nora made a kissing sound and squeezed my shoulder, which felt less like affection than a fact—not, *I like you,* but, *You are the daughter of an old friend.*

I knew there was some appropriate thing my mother wanted me to say, but I couldn't remember what and just offered the standard, "Thank you for having me."

She said, "Thank you for coming," which came out *cubbing;* Aunt Nora suffered from allergies.

I said, "You're welcome," and asked where my parents were sitting; she pointed.

As a judge, my father was an expert at making his face blank, but I could tell he didn't like the man who was talking to him. I cruised right over.

I heard the man say, "Am I right, or am I right?" and then my father noticed me and excused himself from their conversation.

In a low voice, he said, "How's it going?"

"Bad," I told him. "Very bad."

He stood up and put his arm around my shoulders; he walked me away from the table and said, "Want to dance?"

The band was playing "The Impossible Dream"; I said, "This one's kind of schmaltzy."

He said, "Do you know what schmaltz is?"

"I thought I did."

"Chicken fat," he said. He told me that people spread it on bread, and we needed to go to a Jewish restaurant so I could try some.

I said, "Could we go right now?"

He took my hand, and I let him move me around to the chicken-fatty music.

Back at the table, he told me to take his chair and went off to find another, leaving me between Mr. Am-I-Right? and the actress my mother had become.

"Hel-lo," she said, with the two-beat singsong of a doorbell. To the table, she said, "This is my daughter, Sophie."

"Hi," I said.

My mother said, "Are you having a good time?"

I said, "I am having a great time," and then just loud enough for her: "Everyone is more dressed up than I am."

Her smile disappeared, my goal.

She didn't realize that I was kidding until I suggested we drive around and look for tights.

My dad pulled up a chair, and he and I sat very close.

I asked if he was finished with his lunch.

He said, "Go ahead, sweetheart."

I snuck what was left of my father's chicken into a napkin when Aunt Nora came to the table and got everyone's attention: Did anyone want to dance "The Hokey Pokey"? My mother did. She and Aunt Nora walked off with their arms linked.

I spotted them with Rebecca on the dance floor as I made my get-away. The bandleader was singing, "Put your right foot in, and shake it all about," and the three of them did it along with everyone else, without thinking, as I did, *Why? Why would you put your right foot in and shake it all about?*

In the parking lot, I let Albert out of the station wagon and poured water into his bowl. "You're feeling sorry for yourself," I said, feeding him the leftover chicken, "but you don't know how lucky you are."

I was fastening his leash when I heard a voice say, "Hey."

It was the boy who looked like Eric Green.

I said, "Hi."

"I'm Danny," he said. "You don't have a cigarette, do you?"

"Oh," I said. A bunch of girls in my grade had tried smoking at a Girl Scout overnight, but I never had. I looked around the parking lot; we were alone. I said, "There might be a pack in the glove compartment." There was. "I don't see any matches, though."

"I have matches," he said. I handed him two cigarettes, and he held one and put the other behind his ear like a pencil.

He walked with me and Albert past the cars and along the grassy edge of the parking lot. He ran his hand along the bushes. I thought of the one afternoon Eric Green had walked me home from school, his finger through my back belt loop.

Now, Danny said, "Poodles are really smart, right?"

"I can't speak for the whole breed," I said, "but Albert is a genius."

"Can he do tricks?"

"Tricks are beneath him." I said that he'd been named for both Albert Einstein (Robert's hero) and Albert Camus (Jack's).

The sun was glinting off the cars, and in the bright light I saw that this boy looked less like Eric Green than I'd thought. It occurred to me that Danny was older, and I was right.

He told me that he was in eighth grade and his private school had already started. It always started early, he said bitterly, adding that he'd had to miss the last day of hockey camp.

I almost said, *That's too bad,* but it sounded like gloating.

As we walked, the bushes thinned out, and you could see a field on the other side. At a large gap, there was a path and Danny said, "You want to . . . ?" and I said, "Okay."

He took Albert's leash and cut through first. Then he reached his hand out for me. I took it, and he steadied me so I wouldn't slide down the hill, which was more mud than grass.

He said, "You okay?"

I nodded.

He seemed reluctant to let go of my hand, and when he looked at me, everything tingled—not the tiny on-and-off sparks of a foot falling asleep but single and continuous like flying in a dream.

The grass had been mashed down into a path. What had looked like a beautiful field turned out to be a vacant lot; a ratty blanket and rusted beer cans surrounded the ashes and burned sticks of an old campfire. Even so, the sun was lighting up the trees and weeds and flowers. There was the buzzing hum of insects in unison, loud and then quiet.

Danny lit his cigarette and said, "I can't believe summer's over," and I heard in his voice what I knew I'd feel in another week when my school started; it made summer seem less real now.

Danny blew a smoke ring. "Are you going out with anybody?"

I thought again about Eric Green, who had stopped talking to me. "Not at the moment."

At my feet, Albert was sniffing at what looked like a big finger of the flesh-colored gloves Jack wore while dissecting sharks in the basement.

I could feel Danny's eyes on me, and though we were in the shade, I thought of Robert saying that my dress was see-through in the sun. I suddenly felt queasy and nervous. "We should get back."

He didn't move; maybe he was hoping I'd change my mind. He used his first cigarette to light his second.

I got my voice to sound normal, but I felt the quiver underneath when I said, "Come on," to Albert.

I tried to pretend I wasn't hurrying, but I was, and Danny followed. Then we weren't on the path anymore; there wasn't a path. I was stomping down weeds. Pricker bushes were scratching my legs. Finally, I caught sight of the parking lot through the weeds. We'd wound up behind the synagogue, where only a catering truck and a maintenance van were parked.

I slowed down a little then; we walked side by side. In the distance, I could see guests leaving. A few wild children were running around while their parents talked. Rebecca's father, carrying a tutu centerpiece, was helping her grandmother into a sedan. I saw my father then; he was smoking near the station wagon.

On reflex, I crouched down behind a Cadillac, and Danny crouched with me. "That's my father," I said.

After a few minutes, Danny said, "You want me to see if he's still there?" He stood up. "What does he look like?"

"Tall," I said. "He's wearing a dark gray suit."

"I don't know."

I stood up. We were safe.

At the station wagon, I noticed that Albert's paws were muddy, and I wiped them with a rag.

Danny took the rag and wiped the mud off my sandals and pulled a blade of grass out from between my toes.

When he opened the door to the synagogue for me, I thought he was going to ask for my address so he could write to me, but all he said was, "Thanks for the cigarettes."

I was relieved and then disappointed.

In the hall, Alyssa rushed up to him and said, "My dad's here." She glared at me. I wondered if she was his girlfriend, or wanted to be; it was one or the other.

Danny didn't seem to care that she was angry. He said, "See ya," to me, and followed her out to the parking lot.

Downstairs, in the pink palace, Robert and Jack were sitting with my father at a table that had been cleared of everything, including the centerpiece.

My father said, "Let your mother know we're going, please," and I walked over to where she stood with a woman wearing a big-brimmed straw hat with a beige ribbon.

"This is my daughter, Sophie," my mom said, in her fakest voice of the day.

The woman said, "And how old are you?"

"Twelve," I said.

She cooed at this impressive accomplishment. "And when is *your* bat mitzvah?"

I was about to say that I wasn't having one when my mother cut in and said, "We're just planning it now."

I was shocked to hear my mother lie, but I didn't give her away. I remembered a cliché that seemed to fit: "Rebecca will be a hard act to follow."

The woman tittered, and said, "She's darling."

. . . . .

At the car, my mother told me to sit up front and didn't speak again until we were on the highway. "Where were you?"

"Walking Albert," I said.

"She was walking Albert," Robert repeated, in my defense.

Without turning around, my mother said, "I'm talking to Sophie, Robert." To me, she said, "You were gone for over an hour."

I was wondering what she suspected, and then I realized that she didn't suspect anything, she was just angry that I'd disappeared. "It wasn't like anyone missed my company," I said. "No one at my table would even talk to me."

She said, "That's not the point."

We passed three exits before she told me what her point was. I was a guest, she said; I was a member of this family. She kept talking, but whatever she was angry about wasn't making it into her lecture.

I knew that eventually I would have to say I was sorry, even if I didn't know why I should be and wasn't. Until I said it, my mother would go on talking and get angrier until she became tired and hurt, at which point my father would take over.

"I'm sorry," I said.

My mother kissed me. "I know you are."

It felt a little less crowded up front then. My mother said what a wonderful job Rebecca had done and then, almost to herself, said she hadn't even started to plan my bat mitzvah.

I looked at my mother. I looked at my dad. It had all been de- cided. I couldn't argue; I was supposed to be remorseful.

At a gas station, I climbed into the way back with Albert, where I closed my eyes and thought about Danny. I didn't remember being queasy or afraid. I remembered him taking my hand. I thought of him saying, "I can't believe summer's over," which I heard now as a decla- ration of love.

· · · · ·

I came home from my first day of getting lost at Flynn Junior High to the news that I had been enrolled in the Hebrew class required of the bat-mitzvah bound. My mother was relieved; she'd been afraid we were too late, but there was room for me after all.

The topic that night at dinner was varsity football. Jack wanted to join the team. We were all surprised. He took photographs and painted pictures; he wrote stories and acted in plays; he'd played soc- cer, but only intramurally.

My parents objected—he would be too busy applying to college, they said—but Jack argued with reason and passion. For example, he said that joining the football team would demonstrate that he was well-rounded, etc., and might even strengthen his applications.

My father seemed glad to give in, and I thought now might be the right time to discuss the bat mitzvah I did not want to have. But his good mood shone down on Robert; my father suggested they hit at the public courts after dinner.

Robert got so excited that he jumped up from the table to change and was on the stairs when my mother said, "Robert?"

He stopped. "May I please be excused?"

My mother said, "Yes," and took this opportunity to ask me to get their cigarettes. She didn't like to ask in front of Robert, who regularly talked to my parents about their imminent smoking-related deaths.

They were supposedly limiting themselves to three cigarettes a day, the best and last of which they smoked together after dinner, with their coffee. They'd switched to Carlton 100s so they'd enjoy smoking less. And they kept them in the basement; the inconvenience was supposed to make them more aware of each cigarette, but I didn't see how, since the inconvenience was all mine.

I thought of this tonight and every night I went down the basement stairs and into what we still called the playroom even though we never played anything in there anymore except the rare game of Ping-Pong. The net was still up, but the table's identity was otherwise concealed beneath the junk that overwhelmed the rest of the playroom.

The cigarettes were stored in the refrigerator of my cardboard kitchen, and to get there I had to step over Jack's barbells and around boxes and books crowned with such unstackable items as an old telephone with its cord cut. Only my kitchen was left uncluttered and intact, which made me wonder if my mother hoped that one day I'd go back to whipping up imaginary cakes and pies for her and my father.

Upstairs, everyone was out on the porch, my parents on a chaise apiece and my brothers in the love seat, leaving an armless chair for me. None of the porch furniture was comfortable, though; it was metal, and when we stood up its diamond pattern was imprinted on the backs of our thighs like fishnet stockings.

Robert had changed into whites, but the excitement he'd had about playing tennis was gone; he sat silent and grim, all of his attention on the two cigarettes I'd put on the table between my parents.

When my father reached for his, Robert closed his eyes and said, "I can't watch this." His voice was matter-of-fact, as it always was, even when he discussed his future as an orphan.

My mother said a sympathetic, "Would you like to be excused?"

He nodded and rose, leaving his chocolate pudding behind in protest, and Albert followed him inside.

My father lit my mother's cigarette and then his. As though in reverie, he held the burned match a moment before putting it in the clamshell that served as an ashtray. I watched him take another puff, and then I began. I said, "I've decided not to have a bat mitzvah."

My father turned to look at me, one hand behind his head in a futile attempt at comfort. He was used to people pleading their cases before him, and he waited for me to plead mine.

Jack seemed amused, so I tried to pretend he wasn't there. He'd become a less reliable ally over the summer, when he'd begun to see himself less as a camper than a counselor, less the oldest child than the youngest parent.

My mother glanced from me to my father. I'd been fighting with her lately as I never had before—twice that week I'd sent her down to the cardboard refrigerator—and though she'd told my father, he had yet to witness this behavior himself. It occurred to me that she hoped he would now.

I kept my voice calm. "The only reason I'd do it would be for material gain." With a pang, I thought of the stereo my parents had given Jack for his bar mitzvah. "In conclusion," I said, "this seems wrong."

My father nodded for me to go on.

I thought, *Did you not hear my "in conclusion"?* But I nodded myself, as though deciding which of my many powerful points to voice next. "I don't know what I believe in," I said. "So I don't think I should go up on a stage and act like I do."

Robert's voice came from behind the screen door: Softly, less to us than himself, he said, *"Beema."* He knew the correct term for the stage in a synagogue because, unlike Jack and me, Robert had gone to Hebrew school since kindergarten. He loved it. The only reason he wasn't going this year was that he'd been chosen to tutor fifth-graders less brilliant than himself.

We all turned to look at him, a small figure in white.

He said, "Do you know what cilia are?"

My father sighed. "We're having a conversation here, honey."

Robert had written to the American Cancer Society and the American Lung Association for help, and often quoted from the brochures they'd sent. "Cilia are little hairs that keep your lungs clean," he said now. "When you smoke, you paralyze them."

My mother said, "Why don't you come out and finish your pudding?"

"Did you hear what I said?" Robert asked.

"We heard, honey," my father said and turned back to me, my cue to continue. I thought of saying, *Having a bat mitzvah represents everything I stand against.* But I knew my father would say, *For instance?* and I hadn't prepared examples. I was working up the courage to say, *My decision is final,* when my mother spoke.

If she'd wanted my father to witness my defiance a moment earlier, I could see that she didn't now. "You used to love Hebrew school," she said.

I said, "That was in first grade." It was true that I'd loved my teacher, Miss Bell, and songs like "Let My People Go," and stories about jealousy; but it was also true that I'd been so little that when Miss Bell had talked about God as Our Father, I'd pictured mine.

The four of us were looking at my father now. All that was left was for him to deliver his verdict. I didn't know what he would say. He could surprise you, because he really was fair.

He said, "I'd like to talk to Sophie alone," and Jack and my mother got up and followed Robert inside.

My father's cigarette was down to the filter now, and he took the last possible puff. In his face I saw that he was sorry about that; maybe he was already thinking of all the hours that separated him from his next cigarette.

He said, "You seem to have made up your mind."

I barely managed to say, "I've given it a lot of thought."

"Have you?" he said. "It's a big decision to make on your own."

I said, "I can understand that," which didn't sound right, and I realized that I'd just repeated a phrase he often used during discussions.

He looked right at me and said, "Having a bat mitzvah is an important part of being Jewish."

In his voice I heard the unexpected magnitude of my decision: It separated me not just from my mother but from him, too, and maybe even from my brothers. I thought of the story of Moses parting the Red Sea for the Jews, and I saw my family safe on the far shore, waving as I drowned with Pharaoh's soldiers in the unparting sea.

As though underwater, I could barely hear my father's words.

He said that a bat mitzvah was a rite of passage into adulthood. "I still remember mine. I didn't like studying for it," he said. "No one does."

I thought, *Robert will.*

My father's voice sounded more normal when he said, "Your bat mitzvah wouldn't have to be like Rebecca's."

He kept his eyes on me. "We won't make any plans until you say so," he said. "But I'd like you to try Hebrew school."

It was more of a request than a command, and I was lulled by his respectful tone. I said, "Okay."

"Good," he said.

Another moment passed before I realized that I'd agreed to go to Hebrew school.

My mother appeared at the screen door. "Would you like a piece of fruit or anything?"

"Yes," he said. "I'd like a cushion for this goddamned chair."

"Maybe next year," she said. Then: "Robert's waiting."

My father looked at me. He said, "Are we finished, sweetheart?" and I said that we were.

· · · · ·

My mother gave me a lift to Hebrew school. She brought Albert along to make me feel better and said that she wouldn't mind a little music, meaning that I could tune the radio to a station I liked.

I said, "Thank you anyway."

We drove in silence. The sun was still strong and the sky a summer blue, and I thought of the vacant lot and of Danny saying, "I can't believe summer's over."

We turned up the long driveway. The synagogue was pretty if I covered my left eye and just saw the old mansion part, where the offices were, and not the ugly new addition—a submarinelike tunnel of classrooms plus the actual temple with its trapezoidal stained-glass windows.

At the entrance, my mother said, "You know, Aunt Nora and I weren't allowed to have bat mitzvahs. They were just for boys."

I turned a blank eye to my mother, informing her that her words were irrelevant to me.

"Well," she said, forcing a smile, "I'll pick you up at five-thirty."

I said my most wretched, "Good-bye."

After I closed the door, she said, "Sophie?" and for a second I thought that maybe she would say something comforting, or even, *I don't want you to suffer: Let's go.* Unlike my father, she was capable of reversals.

She said, "Did you want to thank me for the lift?"

· · · · ·

The classroom was brand-new and modern, with petal-shaped desks, a skylight, and Hebrew letters in fluorescent colors tacked above the blackboard—probably an attempt to make us think that Hebrew was groovy. Instead, the room reminded me of the Muzak version of a rock song. I took the last seat in the last row so I could be closest to the door.

The teacher was writing on a pad and seemed oblivious to the dozen twelve- and thirteen-year-olds who faced him. I exchanged silent greetings with the ones I recognized from regular school, even Leslie Liebman, whose hands were folded on her desk.

The bell rang, and just when it was getting strange for the teacher not to start the class, he stood. He wrote his name on the board and faced us.

Very slowly, he said, "I am Moreh Pinkus."

I'm sure we all thought that *moreh* was his first name and were surprised to hear him say it to us; it wasn't until the second class that we learned that *moreh* meant *teacher* in Hebrew.

He was probably in his early thirties but seemed much older, as the very religious sometimes do. He was almost bald, which made me wonder if he'd glued his yarmulke on. He seemed to shuffle because the trousers of his suit were too long. I would have thought he was Orthodox, but he didn't have long curls in front of his ears or the beard that I thought was required.

After introducing himself, Moreh Pinkus rummaged through his briefcase for what turned out to be the attendance sheet. He read it over, and even then hesitated before speaking; it occurred to me that he didn't trust or like his voice.

He called my name first: "Applebaum, Sophie?"

"Here," I said.

He looked up at me for a long moment, so long I wondered if he'd divined how much I didn't want to be there. But he did the same with the next person and the next—calling the name, studying the face—until he said, "Muchnick, Margie?" and there was no answer.

It seemed possible that she had dropped out or was in the other class, and I hoped that she had or was. Margie Muchnick was one of the girls who lived on or around Foxrun Road—the Foxes, they were called—and though I wasn't one of their main victims, nobody was immune; they'd nicknamed me Sofa and tortured me about Eric Green.

Moreh Pinkus repeated, "Muchnick, Margie?" and she walked in and said, "Here."

Inexplicably, she sat at the desk next to mine.

Margie was short and solid, dressed in a baggy sweatshirt, jeans, and black high-tops. She had a round face and wore her red hair in two bunches, big fat frizz balls. Her eyelashes and eyebrows were almost white, and she had the yellow-brown eyes I imagined a fox might have.

I didn't acknowledge her, let alone mouth, *Hi,* as I had to my other un-friends. I pretended not to see her, just as I did when I ran into any of the Foxes.

There was an embarrassing silence while Moreh Pinkus waited for her to apologize for her lateness; then he looked down at the attendance sheet and read the next name.

To make up for Margie's rudeness, Leslie Liebman helped Moreh Pinkus distribute our *Hebrew I* textbooks.

Margie flipped through the lessons and exercises. "Fascinating," she said.

At the blackboard, Moreh Pinkus wrote out the Hebrew alphabet; slowly, slowly, slowly he said the name of each letter, pronounced the sound it made, and waited for us to repeat after him.

It was hot, and Moreh Pinkus removed his suit jacket and draped it around his chair. When he returned to the board, I saw that he'd missed a belt loop. I noticed, too, that he wore a wedding ring, and I thought it might not be a bad idea for Mrs. Pinkus to look her husband over before he left the house.

I tried to focus on Moreh Pinkus, but it was hard.

Margie pushed her sleeves up, revealing a wristful of baby bracelets—seed pearls interspersed with tiny alphabet cubes on a chain that turned your wrist green—last year's symbol of friendship. I'd lost mine in the ocean, but now, just as Moreh's wedding band revealed that he was married, my bare wrist seemed to announce that I was friendless.

I kept wishing Margie hadn't sat next to me. I wondered if it would attract too much attention for me to change desks.

She herself solved the problem. She had a coughing fit—a loud one—and you could tell it was fake. I thought that she was trying to amuse herself or to get our teacher to turn away from the board. But she was just setting up the pretext for her escape: She left the room, as though in need of water.

I felt better as soon as she'd gone. With the rest of the class, I repeated after Moreh Pinkus, but the Hebrew letters refused to enter my brain. I fell into a bored daze, which I interrupted only to check the wall clock and will its audible minute hand to tick faster.

I pretended to take notes, looking up at the board and down at my notebook, while I wrote out the words to Bob Dylan's "Highway 61 Revisited." I lingered over "God said to Abraham kill me a son/Abe said, 'Man, you must be puttin' me on,'" which seemed pertinent.

It wasn't until I had to go to the bathroom that I realized how long Margie had been gone. *She'll be back in a second,* I thought. I wrote out all the words to "I Shall Be Released," until I was desperate to be released myself. I left the room.

Margie wasn't at the fountain or in the hallway; nobody was. To be safe, instead of going to the bathroom two rooms up, I went to the one across the temple, all the way down the hall, past the classrooms, the lobby, and the gift shop.

I opened the door to the powder room and tried to appear calm when I saw Margie. She was sitting sideways, her legs slung over the arm of one of the fat, maroon velveteen chairs that faced the mirror. "Well hello, Sofa."

I said, "Hi, Margie," and went through the second door, to the stalls and sinks.

I planned to say nothing as I passed back through the powder room on my way out, but she said, "Can you believe this?"

Assuming that she meant the misery that was Hebrew, I said, "I know."

She said, "Do you have any candy or gum?"

"Sorry."

She took out a pack of cigarettes and asked if I wanted one.

I hesitated, but when she handed the cigarette to me I took it, and when she lit the match I leaned forward. I imitated my mother accepting a light from my father and exhaled as she did, ceiling-ward.

Margie held her own cigarette between her teeth like a killer; she was imitating someone, too—maybe the Penguin from *Batman*.

It was fascinating to see myself smoke, but I forced myself to turn away from the mirror in case Margie was observing me. I kept my eyes on the wallpaper, maroon-and-silver ladies with swirls for hair, such as you would see in a Peter Max print. Then, looking at the swirly wallpaper, I felt seasick. I pretended I'd dropped an earring in the shag rug so I could put my head between my legs.

"Did you lose something?" she said.

I couldn't speak.

When I felt better, I fidgeted with my earring and sat up.

I held the Marlboro until it had burned down low enough to be considered smoked and went to throw it in the toilet.

I stood there a moment, relieved to the point of elation: I hadn't gotten caught smoking and hadn't done anything Margie could make fun of or report to the Foxes.

In the powder room, she held out her hand in what I realized was an offer or challenge to thumb wrestle. I sat down again. We clasped fingers. Our thumbs tapped out the requisite side-to-side one-two-three.

Her nimble thumb danced while mine lumbered—hers was a swashbuckler, mine a polar bear. She pinned my thumb down hard.

"Best of three," she said.

I tried to copy her fancy thumb work, but again she won.

After best of seven, I said I was going back to class, and she didn't stop me.

She herself returned at the very end, when Moreh Pinkus was writing our assignment from *Hebrew I* on the blackboard. He faced us and asked if we had any questions.

Without raising her hand, Margie said, "Is this homework?"

He said, "Pardon?"

"We get homework from regular school," she said. "We're not supposed to get any from you." I wondered if this was true—I hoped it was—but it seemed more likely that it was just another coughing fit.

"If you wish to learn Hebrew," he said, in his interminably slow voice, "you will need to study."

He dismissed us with a formal, "Shalom," and a few of us mumbled shy shaloms back.

Margie walked outside with me, where all our mothers waited in station wagons. When she found hers, she turned to me and said, "See you 'round, basset hound."

· · · · ·

At dinner, my father said, "Well? Was it the torture you thought it would be?"

I said, "Worse," and was ready to elaborate. I was hoping that if I told the truth, he would say that he was glad I'd given Hebrew school a try, which was what he'd finally said about tennis.

I could tell that he was both let down and a little angry; his eyes got tired, as they did when he looked over my report cards.

Robert rescued me by describing his first day of tutoring Doug Sloane, who'd been held back two grades; Robert imagined out loud how hard that would be.

It would be impossible, I thought, *because you are a genius and Doug Sloane is mentally retarded.*

Jack said that Doug's older brother, who'd also been held back, was on the football team. This led to a description of a catch that Jack himself had made off of what he called "a long bomb" in practice. He drew a diagram of the play on a napkin we passed around.

My father turned back to Robert. "So you think it was wrong for Doug to be held back?"

Robert said, "I feel sorry for him."

"I can understand that," my father said. "But didn't what you learned in fourth grade prepare you for fifth?"

For a while, they debated how the educational system might best serve Doug, and then Robert turned to me. "You know Doug Sloane, right?" Robert knew I did; he was just trying to include me in the conversation.

My mother jumped in: "Does anyone have any idea how high the adult illiteracy rate in this country is?" I doubted she herself knew. Like me, my mother didn't learn facts or acquire knowledge; instead, she had feelings—insecurity about not being knowledgeable, for example.

She looked around the table; none of us knew how high the adult illiteracy rate in this country was.

She said, "Seventeen percent."

I thought, *Eighty-five percent of statistics are made up on the spot.*

. . . . .

I hardly saw Margie in regular school. Flynn Junior High was huge compared to Surrey Elementary, and we didn't have any classes together. The first time I ran into her in the hall, she said a solemn, "Shalom," and I could tell by the way her Fox friends laughed that they thought she was imitating me instead of Moreh Pinkus.

Once, during her lunch and my math period, I looked out the window and saw her sitting on the high wall in the courtyard; the rest of the Foxes were stretched out single file, sunbathing, their shirts pulled up to get their tan stomachs tanner. Margie stood and said something that sounded like, "Good-bye, cruel world," and jumped down and landed hard. None of the Foxes even sat up.

. . . . .

Unlike the other Hebrew-school teachers, Moreh Pinkus did not give us a break halfway through class; when Margie suggested it, he misunderstood and said, "Please use the restroom whenever you need to." She left class immediately, and returned only to leave again.

Moreh Pinkus went through the Hebrew alphabet, but now the class called out each letter's name and pronunciation without his assistance. I seemed to be the only one who hadn't memorized the alphabet, the only one who'd forgotten to do the homework, the only one who hadn't learned the vocabulary words. It was just the second week, and I was already the Doug Sloane of the class.

When Margie came back to the room, I left.

In the hall, I heard my name and turned around. It was my first-grade teacher, Miss Bell.

I was thrilled that she remembered me.

She told me that she didn't teach anymore; she assisted the rabbi now. She was on her way to his study, and I walked with her.

I said, "Do you like your new job?"

She said, "I miss students like you."

When she asked who my teacher was and how I liked Hebrew, I remembered my father's disappointment in the truth. I told Miss Bell that Hebrew and Moreh Pinkus were great.

Then she took a left through the temple and I took a right to the powder room. I was washing my hands when the door banged open, and Margie said, "Get a paper towel."

On it, she drew the blanks and noose for hangman.

I didn't mind playing; what I minded was not having a choice. I was better at hangman than thumb wrestling. Margie hung herself again and again. Still, she kept saying, "One more." When I got up to go, she offered me the rest of her cigarettes if I played one more game.

I did, but I wouldn't take the cigarettes.

"Come on," she said. She told me that she had an endless supply; her parents bought their cigarettes by the carton. She said, "They don't care," which I assumed was her bravado way of saying they wouldn't notice. She pulled a cigarette out for herself and then threw the pack at me.

I caught it almost by accident. "Okay," I said, "thanks," and got up to leave.

"Sophie?"

It was a shock to hear Margie say my real name. It took me back to a time when I hadn't been afraid of her at all—fourth grade, Girl Scouts. I remembered waking up in a tent, and that the clothes I put on were warm because her mother, the troop leader, had told us to put them at the bottom of our sleeping bags.

When I turned around, Margie had a cigarette dangling from each nostril.

· · · · ·

We had a string of Indian-summer days, and everyone hung out in the courtyard. During math, I saw a group of boys, possibly eighth- or even ninth-graders, talking to the Foxes who sunbathed on the wall.

Margie sat at the very end. She was making faces—mimicking the boys—for her own amusement.

The next time I checked the courtyard, I didn't see Margie. Instead I saw Eric Green—or, that is, I caught a glimpse of his blond head. Through breaks in the crowd, I saw that he was walking his bicycle—a white ten-speed Peugeot—but I couldn't see much else until he got to the archway. Then I had a clear sight of him from behind; he had his arm around the narrow back of a girl I didn't know, and one finger through a belt loop of her jeans.

I was almost grateful when the math teacher, Mr. Faye, pulled the shade down and closed the window.

. . . . .

In Hebrew school, Moreh Pinkus called Margie's name twice, as he had that first day, and then marked her absent.

It seemed possible that he hadn't learned any of our names, except those of his star pupils: Mitchell Cohen, a shy genius who reminded me of Robert; and Leslie Liebman, whose hand remained perpetually in the air, the Hebrew word—or, as the class progressed, sentence—pursed in her prissy lips.

When anyone else raised a hand, Moreh Pinkus said a reluctant, "Yes?" But he preferred calling on "Mr. Cohen" or "Miss Liebman," whose answers were guaranteed to be correct.

Those of us who never raised our hands seemed invisible to him. He didn't even look up when I left the room.

I went down the hall to the lobby and browsed at the display case ambitiously called the gift shop, never open. There was nothing in that case I wanted—not the menorahs or the Jewish-themed jewelry, not the illustrated children's books about Jewish holidays or history—but I scanned the case as though it might contain a Bob Dylan album I didn't have or the cross-stitched peasant blouses I liked.

Then into the powder room. I was slouched down in one of the cushy chairs when I heard pounding coming from the bathroom.

I pushed the door open. Margie was trying to get dimes out of the Kotex machine.

"I didn't think you were here," I said.

She said, "I'm not here."

I was impressed that Margie was unwilling to go to class even for the one second it took to say, *Here.* It made her cutting seem more fearless and forthright than mine.

"Do you have anything to eat?" she asked.

I didn't.

When she lit a cigarette for me, I noticed that she still wore her baby bracelets. She was the only one who did. The bracelet of choice now, worn by both girls and boys, was a stainless-steel cuff engraved with the name and serial number of a soldier missing in Vietnam. It was called an MIA bracelet, and my impression was that you had to order it, but from whom? I asked Margie if she knew.

She said, "I don't know what you're talking about," and got up and tried the door to the supply closet. It was locked, but a few minutes later, she got up and checked it again, as though with time and patience the door might open. I didn't understand her fascination with the closet, which I said was probably just where extra paper towels and toilet paper were stored.

"Really?" she said. "Then why do they lock it?"

I said that I was going back to class, and she said, "What for?"

I said, "I am learning the Hebrew language."

On the spot, she invented an excellent nonsense language that sounded as much like Hebrew as Hebrew did.

I answered in kind, mixing in the few real Hebrew words I knew with sound-alikes. At first we were animated and theatrical, but then I got serious. I found myself telling her about seeing Eric Green with his new girlfriend. In made-up Hebrew, I found the words to describe exactly how I felt. It was a relief just to say them.

Margie responded with a jokey, hand-waving argument, and I thought, *Did you not understand the importance of what I just told you?* I reminded myself that I hadn't spoken in English. Still, I had trouble forgiving her.

I stood and said, *"Mishpoka,"* meaning, *See ya,* and she said, *"Mishpoka,"* back.

Then I was out in the hall. I couldn't bring myself to go back to class yet, so I stopped at the gift shop to browse again through all the items I wouldn't want even if they were free.

I started at the sound of Miss Bell's voice: "Aren't you supposed to be in class?"

I turned around and waited for her to recognize me, a student who made her miss teaching.

She just blinked

All I could do was nod, *I'm going,* and go.

I walked up the long hallway back to class. Right before I opened the door, I turned around and saw that Miss Bell was still standing there in the lobby, watching me, her arms folded below her chest.

· · · · ·

When I got home from Hebrew school, Jack was sitting on the kitchen floor reading his favorite novel, *The Stranger,* Albert at his side.

I got down on the floor, too. I said, "I hate Hebrew school."

Jack said, "Everybody does."

I realized that he was home early. "Don't you have practice?"

He acted like he hadn't heard my question, but I'd learned from my father that if you waited long enough, Jack would answer.

Finally, he said, "We had an away game."

I said, "Why aren't you away?"

When he answered, his voice was so quiet I didn't think he wanted me to hear him: "I wasn't going to get to play."

"Why not?"

He raised his voice to normal volume, but it sounded louder because of how quiet it had been. " 'Why?' " he said. "Because I'm not good enough."

I was about to say, *That's not true,* but I realized that it was true; he wouldn't have said it otherwise. I waited a minute, and then I said, "That sucks."

He laughed, which was a relief. Then he said, "Want to watch cartoons?"

"Cartoons?"

He said, "I was just thinking how we never watch cartoons anymore."

I thought, *Did we ever watch cartoons?*

We took glasses of milk and a plate of oatmeal cookies upstairs to the guest room where the television was.

Jack turned the channel to the cartoon *Spider-Man* and said, "It's Spidey."

I said, "We should get a big color television."

He said, "Mom and Dad don't want one," as if I didn't know.

We'd been watching *Spider-Man* for about three minutes when he said, "The problem is that I don't really like cartoons anymore."

"I never liked them." I got up and changed the channel to a *Brady Bunch* rerun. "Why is that a problem?"

His voice got serious. "I guess I'm afraid I'm running out of things I like."

"You like new things," I said. "Like football."

As soon as the words were out I was sorry. I was trying to take them back when I said, "I don't get why you went out for it in the first place."

I waited a long, long time for him to answer. Finally, I put my hand on his bicep, and without a word he flexed it for me.

I asked if he had any ideas about how I could get out of Hebrew school.

He said, "Talk to Dad."

"What should I say?"

"Say it's interfering with regular school."

I'd hardly done any homework since school had begun. "I don't think I can say that."

He studied me for a second. "You should do your homework, Sophie." He turned off the television and went to his room.

I snapped the TV back on, but I was too angry to watch.

At the stairs to his bedroom, formerly our attic, I knocked on the wall.

"Don't come up," he called down.

I said, "I want to talk to you."

He didn't answer.

"Don't tell me to do my homework," I called up. "You're not my father."

He came down the stairs in his sweatpants.

I said, "Did you hear me?"

"I'm not your father," he said.

"Right," I said, following him down to the kitchen.

He said, "Okay," in the tone my father used when he said, *Point taken.*

I stood by while he put on his socks and tied his sneakers.

He was almost out the door when I said the line from *The Sound of Music* I'd repeated each time he'd left to go running that summer: "You can't run away from your problems, Liesl; you've got to face them."

He'd smiled whenever I'd said this before—he appreciated repeating jokes as much as I did, but I could see he didn't appreciate this one anymore; he opened the door and ran down the driveway.

I was helping my mom with dinner when he came back, sweaty and red-faced. He was stretching against the station wagon. I opened the door and, without thinking, made the joke I'd always made upon his return: "I knew you'd come back!"

This time he smiled, so I kept going. I pretended that he'd been gone for years, and he let me hug him. "I told you he'd come home," I said to my mother. "This calls for a celebration!"

· · · · ·

I decided I would talk to my father after dinner; I planned to tell him that I had no Hebrew aptitude and also to convey the message of Bob Dylan's song "It Ain't Me, Babe." Though obviously written about a girlfriend, this song contained the overall message I needed to deliver to my parents: Unfortunately, we all had to face that I was not the person they wanted me to be.

The door to my father's study was open but, as usual, Jack was in there. I decided to wait in the hall. I'd just sat down when I heard Jack say, "It's interfering with my applications."

My dad said, "I don't see any evidence of that."

There was a silence, and I knew he was waiting for Jack to tell the truth.

"I want to spend time with Robert and Sophie," he said, "before I go away."

"That's a nice thought."

"I'm worried about Sophie," Jack said.

"That's not your department, Buddy."

Jack said, "She seems sort of lost."

I thought, *Lost how? How am I lost?* Suddenly I felt lost.

My father said, "You want to quit football to take care of Sophie?" He had a gift for rewording a point so you could hear how idiotic it was. "I thought you liked football."

"I don't know," Jack said. "I don't know what I like." Then he was talking about *The Stranger* and meaninglessness, which was meaningless to me; I considered going upstairs to worry about myself.

My father's voice was gentle, but I could tell he was getting impatient when he said, "Let's save existentialism for another night." Then he asked exactly what I had—why Jack had wanted to go out for the team in the first place—and I thought, *Score one for Sophie,* and maybe I wasn't so lost after all.

Jack waited a long time to answer. "I guess I wanted to be the kind of guy who plays football."

"What kind is that?" my dad said, which was exactly what I wanted to know.

Jack said, "Or I didn't want to be the kind who *can't* play football."

My father said, "What's wrong with being a nerdy Jewish intellectual?" meaning himself.

It was funny just hearing my father use a word like *nerdy,* and I expected Jack to laugh, but he said, "I tried so hard," and the pain I heard in his voice made my stomach hurt.

My father said things like, "You never played before," and, "You made the goddamned varsity," and then they were talking about backup schools, Penn versus Cornell.

I lay down on the rug and studied its repeating rams. It was fraying, and one long string looked very much like it wanted to be pulled. I told myself that if I didn't pull it, my father would let me quit Hebrew school.

I woke to my father saying, "Sweetheart?" and the rough rug on my cheek.

I sat up.

He said, "Did you want to talk to me?"

I nodded, and yawned.

He yawned, too, and asked if it could wait until tomorrow, and I said it could.

But tomorrow was Thursday, his night to play indoor tennis, and Friday he decided to go to services. Robert went with him, acting like it was a big treat. From my window, I watched the two of them walk down our street, my father's hand on Robert's shoulder.

· · · · ·

In math, I could feel how cold and dreary the afternoon was, the drizzle and the gray sky, though I couldn't see it; since our week of Indian summer, Mr. Faye had kept the shades down.

It was the sound of a ball booming against the side of the building that made him go over to the window and lift the shade.

We all turned to look: Margie was out in the courtyard by herself. She was holding a brown-red ball and was about to drop it for another kick when Mr. Faye got the window open.

Before he could speak, she called out, "Sorry."

After Mr. Faye closed the window and pulled the shade down, I remembered Margie playing kickball at Surrey. When she was up, everyone in the outfield would automatically move way out. I'd seen her kick it over the fence for a home run. I remembered her running the bases. Afterward, she'd looked miserable—flushed, sweaty, squinting, winded—but now it occurred to me that she'd been happy.

Hardly anyone played kickball at Flynn, and no girls. I felt sorry

for her then, but I doubt she felt sorry for herself. Mr. Faye had just
returned to the board when another kick boomed against the wall.

· · · · ·

That Wednesday, I brought a Baggie of gingersnaps to Hebrew
school. I knew Margie wouldn't be in class, but I thought she might
be in the powder room, and she was.

She was sitting upside down on the velveteen chair, her head on
the rug, high-tops in the air. She held our sixth-grade graduation
booklet from Surrey, entitled "Memories: The Way We Were."

She asked me to fish her cigarette out of the waste can, and I did,
making sure it hadn't started a fire that would burn the synagogue
down.

When she thanked me for the cookies, her voice had no expression
in it at all, but I assumed this was from the strain of being upside
down.

I wished I could've brought milk, which made gingersnaps taste
better, especially if these were as stale as I suspected. She sat up and ate
them slowly, thoughtfully, softening each bite in her mouth before
chewing.

I sat in the chair next to hers, and she shared the graduation booklet with me. She had it opened to a page on which one of the Foxes
had written, "Don't ever change!" and another, "Foxes forever."

On the opposite page, I caught a glimpse of my own picture and
signature. What I'd written sounded sarcastic now: "Good luck in Jr.
High!"

She said, "I'm glad I kept this," as though the booklet were a cru-
cial piece of evidence that would prove her innocence and the Foxes'
guilt in an upcoming friendship tribunal.

Then she said, "I'm not the one who changed."

I was suddenly enraged. I remembered the Foxes ganging up on
anyone who was alone during recess. I thought of their regular victims: Richie, who was pale and thin, they called "Queer"; Sheralynn,
who was shy, "Weird"; and Charles, who was retarded, "Retarded."

"Sofa" was mild by comparison, and at first I hadn't really minded

their singing, "Sofa and Eric sitting in a tree, K-I-S-S-I-N-G . . ." I'd
even hoped that it would remind Eric of his feelings for me and bring
them back. But when it didn't, the song was torture, as were their
smooching sounds.

I'd known my mother couldn't help; she pronounced *clique* the
French way, CLEEK, and would just tell me that the Foxes were jealous and to ignore them.

I'd gone to my dad. As usual, he'd wanted to know the full story;
he'd wanted to know my part in it. "What do they tease you about?"

I told him they called me weird.

"Oh, sweetheart," he'd said. "The meek shall inherit the Earth."

At the time, I'd heard only the implication that I was meek, which
felt even worse than being called *lovesick* and *Sofa*. But now I remembered how gentle his tone had been, and I wondered if he'd just meant
meek as the opposite of bossy, and if his unspoken message was that
one day the bossy shall fall.

This day seemed to have come for Margie. It had become important to be pretty, and she wasn't; important to have boys like you, and
none liked her. Everyone I knew had dropped out of Girl Scouts. I
was sure all the Foxes had; I doubted the Foxes even thought of themselves as Foxes anymore, except as it meant "sexy ladies."

Margie's thumbs were pushed up against her eyelids—she was
crying—and I was surprised to find myself feeling sorry for her. I tried
to think of something to say. I remembered how happy she'd seemed
in Girl Scouts, wearing her pale green uniform and her dark green
sash with all the badges sewn on it. To earn them, you had to perform
impossible tasks, such as visiting an elderly person for a year; at the
end of my stint in Girl Scouts, I'd safety-pinned exactly three badges
to my sash. Now I marveled aloud at how many she'd earned.

She said, "My sister Joy helped me." Both of her sisters were away
at Penn State now, she said, and hardly ever came home "except for
vacations."

I told her that my brother was going away next year and had already changed.

She said, "Joy got engaged," as though this was the culminating betrayal. A moment later, she added, "His name's *Ted*."

She seemed more forlorn than ever, so I tried to bring the topic back to Girl Scouts. "You know what I liked about the camping trips?"

She handed me another cigarette. "What?"

I didn't have an answer ready; I tried to think of what I had liked. "The outdoors."

She told me that there was a camping trip in a couple of weeks. "You want to come?"

"Can I go if I'm not a Girl Scout anymore?"

"Lee goes." When she saw that I didn't know who Lee was, she said, "Miss King."

Miss King—or Miss K, as some of the girls called her—had played guitar and sung folk songs on our camping trips. She'd always worn the same outfit, jeans and a jean shirt, a suede coat, and old leather boots you'd expect a folksinger to own. She was husky, and her face resembled Arlo Guthrie's and her hair fluffed up like Bob Dylan's. I'd wanted to like her but hadn't; once, after we'd all sung "Blowin' in the Wind," Miss K had told me that I'd been flat.

I said, "But she gets to go because she plays the guitar, right?"

"She goes because she's best friends with my mother," Margie said. "She practically lives at our house."

Later, I would hear that Miss King was in love with Mrs. Muchnick.

Now Margie said, "My dad doesn't like her."

I couldn't picture any friend of my mother's, even Aunt Nora, living with us, and especially one my father didn't like.

"Anyway," she said, "you can come if you want."

"I'll ask," I said, though I knew I wouldn't.

The bell rang then, so I couldn't even go back to class to get my *Hebrew I,* which made me feel like a criminal.

· · · · ·

At dinner, my father said that he had been meaning to ask how Hebrew school was going.

I swallowed. "The same."

He said, "Are you giving it a fair chance?"

I'd forgotten that I was supposed to do more than show up, and, picturing my *Hebrew I* on my desk in the dark classroom, I could hardly get my head to nod.

After dinner, when I was sent to get the cigarettes in the basement, I was glad to be by myself for a minute. I stood in my cardboard kitchen. It had belonged to Rebecca first, and by the time Aunt Nora had given it to me, as a birthday present, it appeared to have undergone years of industrial food preparation. I'd been bitterly disappointed, especially by the stove; it was white with three red concentric circles for burners, and what should have been the fourth was ripped down to its brown corrugated cardboard. I'd stared at the stove incredulously and thought, *I can't cook with this!*

My mother had said, "Did you want to thank Aunt Nora?"

"Thanks."

Right in front of me, Aunt Nora had said, "You're not strict enough with her."

Later my mother had scolded me about my manners. I'd said, "Isn't it bad manners to give a used present?"

She'd said, "Sometimes that can make a present even more special."

· · · · ·

Moreh Pinkus held up my *Hebrew I*, and I took it from him. I didn't know whether to thank him or apologize. I wound up saying nothing.

After attendance, he announced that we would not have class next week, "in observance of Yom Kippur, the Day of Atonement," and though his voice was heavy with the importance of the holiday, I still felt the joy of an unexpected reprieve. I would have clapped if anyone else had, but instead I hid my hands inside the desk, and my fingers performed a merry folk dance.

It seemed possible that the whole class was as thrilled as I was; whenever Moreh Pinkus asked a question, almost everybody raised their hands. It was as though they'd all suddenly turned into Leslie Liebmans, and, as though they had, Moreh Pinkus was calling on all of them.

Then he said, "Please put your books on the floor and take out a pencil."

I thought, *You can't give a test without warning.* But no one else seemed surprised, and I realized that he'd probably announced the test at the end of last week's class, when I'd been in the powder room; he could've announced the test a hundred times and I wouldn't have known, I'd been in class so little.

The first half of the test was Hebrew and the second half English, sixteen sentences in all, each with a blank line underneath for the translation.

I thought, *Did you ever hear of multiple choice?*

When I looked up, he was watching me. He said, "Just do the best you can."

I stared at the test for a long time, and particularly at the sentence "The teacher brought the book to school," and prayed for a divine force to fly the Hebrew translation into my brain.

None came and there was no point in guessing. Finally I decided to write a note:

> DEAR MOREH PINKUS,
>
> I DID NOT HAVE MY BOOK, AND THEREFORE
> COULD NOT STUDY FOR THIS TEST.
>
> SORRY,
> SOPHIE APPLEBAUM

I handed in my test, and left the room, even though I could feel Moreh Pinkus staring at me. I went down the hall to the powder room.

Margie was standing at the closet door. Her cheeks were as flushed as they'd gotten after her home runs, and I noticed her hair was back in a barrette instead of up front in two bunches.

She stepped aside and ceremoniously opened the door to the closet; like a lovely assistant in a game show, she gestured at the shelves lined with plastic-wrapped merchandise from the gift shop.

"It was unlocked?" I said.

She set her woolly hair free and demonstrated inserting the barrette in the lock.

She'd already made a pile on the floor of what she wanted to take—mostly jewelry, but also boxes of multicolored Hanukkah candles and net satchels of gold-foiled chocolate coins. "Check it out," she said, handing me a big plastic bag of jewelry, each piece in its own little bag. I dumped the bag and spread its contents on the counter.

She brought her own stash over to try on next to me.

I found a silver cuff that looked a lot like an MIA bracelet, except it had Hebrew writing where the soldier's name and number belonged.

I looked at my wrist in the mirror, and then I saw all of me and then both of us, and what I saw was the enormity of this crime through my father's eyes: If there was a God, this was about as close as you could get to stealing from Him in the modern world; this seemed so obviously wrong, so symbolically wrong, we might as well have melted the jewelry down and created a golden calf to worship.

But it wasn't God or religion or my father that made me take the bracelet off. It had nothing to do with getting caught or getting in trouble with anyone but me.

I thought, *What am I doing?* and I surprised myself by saying it aloud. As soon as I did, I got this great feeling; it was like I'd been holding my stomach in for a long time—only what I'd been holding in was my personality—and I let it out now.

All Margie said was, "What's your problem?" but she spoke as though she was once again the boss of the world, addressing the Sofa of yesteryear.

She looked at me in the mirror; she was fastening the catch on a Star of David necklace. She was going to wear it.

I said the thought as it occurred to me: "You want to get caught."

"I don't care," she said. "I think my parents are getting a divorce."

I wasn't sure what her parents' divorce had to do with her theft, but I knew it did. Maybe she was getting back at them, or she felt she deserved these stolen goods in return for what was being taken from her.

"I'm sorry," I said, and meant it.

She shrugged. "You don't want anything?"

"No."

She didn't even look up when I left.

Miss Bell was coming down the hall.

Instead of saying hello, she asked if I knew that there was a bathroom right by the classrooms.

"Yes."

"So why don't you use it?"

I said, "This one's nicer."

Her eyes didn't register that I'd answered her question.

It was scary to walk away from her, just as it had been to walk out on Margie, but I was determined: I would be a slave to no person.

In class, a few students were still struggling with their tests. Leslie Liebman was reading her answers with obvious pleasure—she just couldn't get over how correct they all were.

Moreh Pinkus was saying, "Finish up," when Miss Bell appeared at our door. "Pardon me," he said to us, and joined her out in the hall. Everyone turned around to look; Margie was out there, too.

Miss Bell appeared as agitated and angry as Margie appeared calm and bored.

I kept trying to convince myself that I hadn't gotten caught and wasn't in trouble, but I felt I had and was.

When Moreh Pinkus came back in, I was ready for him to lean down and tell me to collect my things. But he walked right past me and only once he was back at his desk caught my eye. He sighed, and asked everyone to pass their tests forward.

. . . . .

That night, my parents announced that they'd smoked their last cigarettes. I got their pack from my cardboard refrigerator, and they made a ritual of running the leftover cigarettes under the kitchen faucet, as they had in the past.

For the next few days, Robert described the triumphant march of my parents' bodies back to health, their blood vessels expanding, their cilia waking up. During dinner, he'd say, "Doesn't everything taste better?" And afterward, "Why don't we all take a brisk walk?"

My father ground his teeth; my mother wrung her hands.

. . . . .

On Yom Kippur, my father wanted to walk to the synagogue, but my mother took too long getting dressed, and it was all worse because they weren't smoking.

Even though we drove, we were late.

The only seats left in the synagogue were in the last row, right behind where Moreh Pinkus sat with his family. My mother sat directly behind him, and I behind his youngest son.

There were four sons, all wearing pin-striped suits like the one Moreh wore each Wednesday. He himself was in a black suit. Mrs. Pinkus wore a silky flowered dress and a purple hat, and her hair hung in a glossy pageboy my mother would later tell me was a wig.

In front of me, the littlest Pinkus was bending his thumb back as far as it could go; he released it, and then bent it back again. Himself his only toy, he did the same with each of his fingers, and then began to experiment with the mobility of his ear.

Pretty soon the novelty of observing the Pinkuses wore off, and the service became like every other one I'd ever gone to. The rabbi, whose black robes reminded me of the ones my father wore in court, did what seemed to be an imitation of God; when he raised his arms to motion for us to sit or stand, his sleeves hung down a little like bat wings. He droned on, and when the word *congregation* appeared in the prayer book it was our turn to drone.

I looked around to see if anyone was atoning. I knew that Leslie Liebman's face probably had atonement written all over it, in fluent Hebrew, but I just saw her from behind, standing with her family.

Jack whispered in my ear, "My kingdom for a Life Saver; pass it down."

I said it to my mother, who opened her pocketbook. She took out the sugar-free mints that she carried around whenever she was trying to quit smoking. They hardly had any taste, but I took one. The slight entertainment it offered my mouth was more than my eyes and ears were getting.

It was then that Moreh Pinkus began mumbling and rocking back and forth in his seat. I must have seen my grandfather do this when I was little because I knew it was how religious men prayed.

My mother appeared almost girlishly embarrassed.

Jack put his mouth to my ear and whispered, "Rock and roll."

I said a very quiet, "Shh."

It occurred to me that Moreh Pinkus might be the only truly religious person in the whole synagogue, the only one who believed and understood everything he was saying. He wasn't even reading from the book.

It was out of respect for Moreh Pinkus that I stopped saying the congregation parts aloud with everyone else. I read them silently. But what did "Hear, O Israel" mean? And "The Lord is one"—how many would He be? This might have moved Israelites in the desert thousands of years ago, but it did not move me here in the suburbs now.

I decided to try atoning. It wasn't hard to think of things I'd done wrong, with Moreh Pinkus rocking right in front of me, or to feel bad, with my father sitting just down the row.

But I couldn't think of how to fix anything, until everyone was saying the mourner's prayer for people who had died. It was in Hebrew, and though I'd heard it many times—it was said in every service—I'd never learned it. The prayer was spelled out phonetically in English, and I read it quietly at first, and then louder. I said it as clearly as I could, remembering my grandfather, and I hoped that my father could hear me.

After the service, Moreh Pinkus stood in the aisle at the end of our row.

"Hi," I said, the only word I had ever spoken to him, except "Here."

He shook my hand with both of his and said, "Gut Yomtov, Sophie."

I wasn't sure whether it was *Yomtov* or *Yuntov,* so I just said, "Thanks," and, "you, too."

My parents were standing there, and though I was afraid of what he might say about me, I said, "This is Moreh Pinkus; these are my parents."

My father said, "Gut Yomtov," exactly as Moreh Pinkus had; my mother's enunciation was so precise and clipped that her "Good *Yuntov*" sounded more like the King's English than Hebrew.

They shook hands, and then Moreh Pinkus rejoined his family.

On the way to the car, my mother said, "That's your teacher?"

"Yes," I said.

"He's Orthodox," she said to my father.

He didn't answer her. To me, he said, "What kind of a teacher is Moreh Pinkus?"

I tried to think of a word that described him. "Meek?" I said.

. . . . .

I was looking for my *Hebrew I* when I heard my mother blow her nose in the kitchen. When I walked in, she was sitting at the table crying. Albert had one paw in her lap.

"What is it?" I said.

She said, "I just love cigarettes so much," and I took her hand, and didn't let go even once she stopped crying.

"You've been a good sport about Hebrew school," she said.

"Mom," I said. "I haven't."

"You went," she said, in my defense. "And you didn't complain about it."

I noticed her use of the past tense and adopted it. "But I wasn't really there."

She said, "You did the best you could," and she seemed to believe I had.

I said, "I've just been going through the motions," using the expression my father had after he'd watched my first tennis lesson.

"Sweetie," she said, "that's what a lot of life is."

In my meaner days, I would've said, *That's what* your *life is,* but I kept quiet.

The next moment, my mother said, "You don't have to go, if you don't want to." I could tell that it pleased her to say this; relieving me of my misery seemed momentarily to relieve her of hers.

I hadn't thought of her as having the authority to make this decision. "Really?"

She nodded.

I said, "I will go one last time."

She said, "You don't have to."

"I know."

. . . . .

I got there before Moreh Pinkus arrived. Leslie Liebman was telling everyone that Margie had robbed the gift shop and had been expelled. Then she noticed me and said, "How's Margie doing?"

I didn't know; I hadn't seen Margie in school. All I could think to say was, "She hated Hebrew school."

Moreh Pinkus arrived, and after a few minutes, he found our tests in his briefcase. He handed them back slowly. He turned my test facedown so no one could see that it was blank except for my note to him and his note back: "Makeup test."

I thought, *Makeup test?* and imagined Moreh Pinkus asking me to take out an eye pencil and lip gloss; it wasn't that funny, but I still wished there was someone in the class I could tell.

At the board, Moreh Pinkus wrote out the correct translations, and I copied them onto my blank test in the manner of a devoted Hebrew scholar.

Afterward, he opened *Hebrew I* to Section II.

I was determined to stay in class for the entire period. It was an act of atonement and a belated attempt to honor the agreement I'd made with my father. It was for my mother, too; if she could endure the torment of withdrawal, I could endure the torment of Hebrew school.

My torment, however, was unexpectedly great. After what seemed like hours, I gave myself permission to take a short break.

When I opened the door to the powder room, I heard, "What took you so long?" As ever, Margie was sitting sideways in the velveteen chair, smoking.

I knew she could get in trouble just for being here, and I was about to ask why she'd come, but I stopped myself. I knew that she was here to say good-bye to me.

She repeated what I'd just heard from Leslie Liebman, adding that Miss Bell had been "a real asshole. She thought you were guilty."

This hurt.

"But Moron Pink-Ass said you weren't a thief."

"He did?"

She said, "Do you have any food?"

I shook my head.

She lit a cigarette for me, and I took it, though I was aware of the trouble I could still get into. She told me that she'd transferred to an alternative school called Susquehanna; her parents had decided the kids at Surrey Junior High were a bad influence.

I asked if her parents were still getting divorced.

She said, "They're going to counseling."

"That's good."

We were quiet, as we'd been for so many minutes and hours in this room. Margie went to the supply closet and turned the knob—for old times' sake, I guess—and it reminded me that Miss Bell could walk in. I got up and threw my cigarette in the toilet. It made a sizzle sound.

I checked to make sure no one was in the hall, and then Margie and I walked out of the powder room together. We said good-bye at the lobby. I wished her luck at Susquehanna, and I walked up the hall, back to class.

She waited until I had opened the classroom door before she shouted, "See ya soon, you big baboon."

Everyone turned to look at me as I took my seat.

I'd heard that the best way to learn a foreign language was just by being in that foreign country, and I told myself that this could happen to me here and now. I listened to the Hebrew spoken all around me and waited for the miracle of comprehension until the bell sounded.

Moreh Pinkus said his standard, "Shalom."

Everyone said it back to him, pretty much in unison.

I looked at Moreh Pinkus for a long moment, and with my face I thanked him for knowing that I was not a thief. Then I was out of class and down the hall, out the door, and in the driveway.

To myself, I said, *Free at last, free at last, thank God Almighty, we are free at last.*

I found our station wagon in the line of cars. Robert had already gotten in the backseat with Albert so I could have the front.

As we pulled out, I watched the other kids finding their cars, and I thought, *Shalom, suckers.*

Robert resumed the conversation he'd been having with my mother. He was saying that no matter how hard he tried, he couldn't help Doug Sloane understand fractions. "I think he just wants me to do his homework."

Then, abruptly, Robert stopped talking.

My mother didn't seem to notice; she was driving even more slowly than usual, looking in the windows of a house, which she said gave her ideas about decorating.

When I turned around, Robert was staring at me.

"What?" I said.

He shook his head.

At home, he went upstairs without taking his jacket off. He was waiting for me in my room when I got there, and he closed the door after me.

"I know," he said.

When I breathed in, my chest was icy. I said, "Know what?"

"I know you've been smoking," he said. "I smelled it in the car."

I tasted the cigarette on my breath. "I was just trying it."

"Don't lie to me," he said. "This is a matter of life and—" I thought he was going to say "breath," like the TV commercial against smoking, but he said "death." His face was as grave as it had been at our grandfather's funeral.

He asked how much I smoked and with whom and where, and I told him.

When I said Margie's name, he nodded, and to himself he added, "From Girl Scouts," and, "one of the Foxes." Robert remembered everything I ever told him.

After I answered his questions, I told him about Margie robbing the gift shop and getting expelled; I repeated what she'd said about her parents getting divorced and Miss King living at their house. It was a relief to tell him, even though he was just my little brother.

"Well," he said, sounding like the sheriff in a Western, "I don't think you'll be spending much time with Margie Muchnick anymore." Then he said, "Where do you keep your cigarettes?"

I opened the bottom drawer of my desk, and Robert took the pack of Marlboros Margie had given to me.

I said, "Are you going to tell Mom and Dad?"

He said, "I will if I have to." He said he would do anything to get me to stop smoking. "I will make your life miserable," he said, and I knew that he would.

THE TOY BAR

VENICE LAMBOURNE was famous the way a beautiful girl can be in a small circle of places and parties, but hardly anyone knew her. *Knockout* was the word people used to describe Venice, and *bombshell,* and she did seem to stir violence; men could seem almost angry at her for being so pretty.

I met Venice when we were both eighteen. She was my roommate. This was at Rogers, the not-very-good school in Klondike, New York—according to *Barron's Profiles of American Colleges,* median SAT: 1100, average GPA: 2.9. Venice said the reason she was there was that her SATs had somehow not arrived at the better schools she'd applied to; she said that her application to Rogers consisted of one phone call her uncle placed to the admissions committee. I doubted the story, as I did almost every story Venice told, but it turned out to be true—or true enough.

Venice didn't arrive until the night before classes started, hours after the last parents had kissed their freshman sons and daughters good-bye and gotten into station wagons headed homeward for Darien, Connecticut, or Katonah, New York, or, in my parents' case, Surrey, Pennsylvania. Venice pulled up in a cab and carried her sole suitcase inside.

She knocked on what at that moment became our door and walked into what still felt to me like my room.

She was very thin and very tall—five foot ten in flat shoes. She almost always wore flats, one pair until they wore out, and then she'd get another. She didn't have many things—not many clothes or many possessions, either; she believed in owning only perfect things, or, as she said, "one perfect thing."

Her hair was blond and straight, and she tucked it behind her ears; she had blue eyes that you noticed partly because her brows were so dark and thick.

She said, "I'm Venice Lambourne," and when she shook my hand her formality unnerved me so much that I answered as I'd been instructed to as a child: "How do you do?" Then I said, "I'm Sophie. Applebaum."

She told me that she'd been traveling and was exhausted; she'd come all the way from Antibes.

I hadn't heard of Antibes but vaguely remembered a movie called *Raid on Entebbe*, and was it in Israel or somewhere in Africa? Was Israel in Africa?

"Wow," I said, and then suggested that maybe she wanted to check in with our resident adviser, a button-nosed teddy bear named Betsy, who'd been worried.

This Venice seemed not to hear. "I need a drink," she said.

When I told her about the soda machine in the basement, she turned and looked at me as though I was the last and possibly the longest leg of her trip.

She'd passed a bar that she said was close and open. "Those might be its only virtues," she said, "but they are the only virtues I care about at the moment."

I hesitated; with the lack of self-knowledge I'd exhibit for years to come, I'd signed up for an eight o'clock class.

I told her that the bar was called the Pines, and it was the college bar, basically the only bar, but fine; I was hoping that if I talked long enough she'd realize how tired she was.

She raised her thick eyebrows, asking why I was talking about a bar we should be walking to, and I said, "I have an eight o'clock class."

She said, "I don't even know what I'm taking," and won.

It took her about thirty seconds to get ready. She didn't change her clothes—a robin's-egg-blue boatneck, white capris, and black flats, each a perfect thing—and didn't wear makeup, herself a perfect thing. All she did was wash her face.

As we were leaving the room, she noticed my fiddle in its case. "Do you play the violin?"

"I fiddle," I said, and I felt the way I sometimes had when I was little and needed to defend my younger brother from someone older than both of us and hoped I could.

Sort of jokey, she said, "Will you fiddle for me some time?"

"Probably not," I said.

· · · · ·

The Pines was packed. We worked our way up to the bar, where we stood drinkless, waiting for one of the busy bartenders. Standing there, I said aloud what I'd been noticing all weekend: "Does everyone seem unusually good-looking to you?"

She looked around. "No."

I thought maybe her *no* was retaliation for my *probably not*. I said, "The reason I said I wouldn't play my fiddle for you . . . I don't really play for anyone."

"Why not?"

I didn't want to tell her that I wasn't good enough to play for anyone, so I made my face look like I was pondering the question until one of the bartenders came over to us. He was an older guy who turned out to be the owner. "What can I get you girls?"

"Hello," Venice said.

The man's expression didn't change.

"I've been traveling all day," she told him, "so I need something really, really good."

All around us other student drinkers were waiting to order.

She said, "What kind of red wine do you have?" But right away, she said, "No," and again, "No." "Cassis?" she said to herself. "Campari?" As far as I knew, she was naming towns that surrounded Entebbe.

She brightened: Something fruity might revive her—a piña colada, maybe, or a daiquiri. Did he use fresh fruit? He didn't.

"Maybe bourbon," she said. Could he make a mint julep?

He knew his customer now and said, "I don't have mint."

"No mint," she repeated, but she agreed to it, with a sigh, as though she was to face many deprivations here that had been previously unknown to her.

I asked for a White Russian, the drink I'd ordered at bars on the New Jersey shore, where I'd bused tables that summer.

She looked at me like we'd been disagreeing and now she suddenly saw my point. "Two," she said, and the bartender spilled out the bourbon he'd already poured into a glass.

I paid for our drinks—she said she'd used up her dollars on the cab and had only francs and lira—and while I was waiting for my change, I noticed one guy looking in our direction. He said something to the guys he was with, and they looked over, too.

We'd barely sat down when one of them came over to us.

"Hi," he said. He was cute and, like so many students at Rogers, blond; only Scandinavia could claim a higher blond-to-brunette ratio.

"Hi," I said.

He asked if we were freshmen, and I said we were, and I might as well have said, *You can kiss me if you want to.*

Then Venice jumped in, introducing both of us, and I understood that she was being efficient rather than friendly, and he did, too; introducing himself, he seemed slightly crestfallen.

Once she'd learned his name, she used it: "Tad," she said and told him how tired she was and that she'd been traveling all day and would he please forgive her?—she was incapable of conversation.

"Sure," he said. "Absolutely."

But he didn't go, maybe because his crowd of friends was watching. He said, "Where are you coming from?"

She looked at him for a long moment, a reprimand, before saying, "Antibes."

His "wow" had more bravado in it than mine, but I could tell he was a fellow untraveler when he immediately turned the conversation back to the world he knew: "Where are you living?"

Venice had given him a chance to exit gracefully, and he was not taking it; now she answered in the perfunctory manner of filling out a form: "Bancroft."

"Nice," he said. "Bancroft is nice."

She looked away from him to me, a signal to resume our conversation. He was looking at me, too, now, for help. It was hard for me not to give it to him, but I could see that this was between them, and my role was auxiliary—I was the nurse and she was the doctor; I was the nanny and she the mother.

"Well," he said.

She said, "It was nice to meet you, Tad."

"Likewise," he said.

I felt bad for him when he walked away and said, "He seemed kind of nice."

Venice didn't respond. She closed her eyes, and I thought that she really must be tired, and that Tad had made her even more tired, and that soon we would go home, and I would have a chance of waking up for my eight o'clock class and becoming the good student I'd always meant to be.

But when she opened her eyes, her face was dreamy instead of sleepy. Almost to herself, she said, "This morning I was in Antibes," and I thought, *I'm going to be here all night.*

. . . . .

It was after one when we got back to Bancroft. We undressed with our backs to each other, and I noticed that hers was evenly brown from her shoulders to her underpants—no hint of where a bathing suit top might've been, and I wondered if she'd just pulled the straps down and unhooked the back or if she'd gone without.

We were in our beds when I looked over and saw that all that separated her from the mattress was a beach towel. She was using shirts for a blanket. I said, "You want a sheet or something?"

"I'm fine," she said. "Thanks." She explained that she'd mailed her bedclothes from Italy a month before, and they were probably waiting for her at the post office. "But," she added, "you know how slow the mail from Italy is."

No, I didn't, and it kept me from offering her my top sheet and bedspread.

We said good night, and I turned off my light.

In the dark, though, it occurred to me that she was probably the only freshman whose parents hadn't brought her to school. I wondered if that bothered her. I wondered if her parents were having too much fun in Antibes to leave and help her get ready for school and buy her sheets and connect her speakers and meet the other parents. I found myself feeling sorry for her.

I turned the light back on, and we made her bed. I had only one pillow but two cases, and I offered to stuff the spare with socks.

Her voice was smaller than it had been and apologetic when she said, "Do you mind if I sleep with your husband?"

I stared at her. It took me a minute to realize that she meant my reading pillow—it was corduroy with arms—and as I handed it to her, I said, "Did you make that up?"

She said, "That's what it's called."

It would be another year before I told her that at that moment I'd thought she was a split-personalitied nymphomaniac. After that, out of nowhere, she'd sometimes put on a twisted, sexed-up voice and say, "Do you mind if I sleep with your husband?"

I turned off the light again, and we said good night, but then she was saying my name—not addressing me, but musing. "Sophie. It's a pretty name," she said.

"I was named after my great-grandmother," I said.

She said, "It's old-fashioned," which was what I hated about my name. "You don't hear it too often."

"What about yours?" I said, though I wasn't sure what I meant.

She said, "I was named for the place of my conception," and it sounded like she was claiming that the city had been named for her.

But then she said, "I'm lucky they didn't name me Gondola. Or Canal," and I went all the way from hating to liking her, and the distance made me feel like I loved her.

. . . . .

Those first weeks, Venice caused a big stir. I'd go to parties with her—we traveled in packs of at least five or six to fraternities—and once we got there she was always surrounded.

But there were nights when she'd say, "Let's not go," and she'd act like we were cutting a class.

Usually we stayed in to watch a movie on television, a movie she said I absolutely needed to see—*12 Angry Men, The Shop Around the Corner, The Best Years of Our Lives.* We'd go down to the basement TV lounge and turn off all the lights. It would be dark except for the TV and the red of the soda machine and its everlasting NO CHANGE light.

I loved all of the movies she did, and *The Heiress* so much that I forgot all about Venice until the commercials, when she'd repeat the lines she liked best.

Her favorite came at the end of the movie: Years after standing Catherine up on the night they're supposed to elope, Morris comes back, and he's knocking and then pounding on her door, and she says to her servant, "Bar the door, Maria."

" 'Bar the door, Maria,' " Venice said. "The rallying cry of jilted women everywhere."

· · · · ·

In her closet, Venice kept a bottle of Shooting Sherry, just a regular medium-dry sherry, but its name made me think of hounds and horses, plaid blankets, and roaring fires. Some nights after studying we'd drink it out of glasses she'd taken from the dining hall. We'd lie on our beds and talk. I'd smoke cigarettes.

She'd talk to me about a book she'd read for a class—she kept up with her reading, as I never could—or she'd mention an article from the *New York Times*, which she read every day, as no one else did. Or she'd read aloud from a novel she was crazy about; that fall it was *Lolita*, and in the winter *Anna Karenina*.

· · · · ·

Venice didn't confide in me for a long time, and even when she did, it sounded less like a confidence than just a story she wanted to tell because it was interesting.

The first one she told me was about Georges. Their families had rented the villa together in Antibes; he'd come for the last week. As she spoke, I realized it was Georges she'd been thinking of that first night in the Pines when her voice got dreamy and she'd said, "This morning I was in Antibes."

"He's incredibly smart," she said. "But sweet, too. That's rare, I think."

I thought of Doug, the busboy I'd made out with on my last night of work, and it occurred to me that he was not particularly smart and not that sweet, either. "Yeah," I said.

Georges had beautiful manners. "He always stands when a woman enters the room," she said. "I love that kind of thing."

"Me, too," I said, because suddenly I did love that kind of thing, though I wasn't sure I'd ever seen a guy my age stand for a woman unless he happened by coincidence to be leaving at that moment.

Venice told me that Georges spoke six languages fluently, and though English was one of them, the lovers spoke French.

She said that they didn't sleep together until the last night, and she closed her eyes, remembering.

"What?" I said.

She repeated something he'd said to her in French.

I told her that it sounded romantic but I spoke zero foreign languages.

She said, "He kept saying, 'Please don't sleep,' and every time I'd doze off, I'd wake up to him saying, 'Don't sleep, my love. Don't leave me before you have to.'"

"Wow," I said.

She said, "I know."

Maybe she could tell I doubted the story because she got his powder-blue aerograms out, and line by line she read and translated his romantic French.

"Wait," I said. "*Ma puce* means 'darling'?"

She told me that, literally translated, *ma puce* meant "my flea," but, "It's like our 'honey'—no one thinks of actual honey."

I got her to give me the literal translation for every "darling" or "sweetheart": *Mon chou* meant "my cabbage," *mon lapin,* "my rabbit."

After she told me about losing her virginity to a Swiss ski instructor, she looked over at me. I knew she was waiting for me to tell her my story, and it occurred to me to make one up. Instead, I admitted that I'd never skied.

· · · · ·

Our resident adviser invited Venice and me into her homey room, saying, "I just want to have a little chat." She asked if we wanted tea or coffee, and she also had hot chocolate and chicken noodle soup.

I was sort of excited at the idea of chicken noodle soup. "I'll have some soup," I said. "Thanks."

Venice gave me a look: *Let's not make this any longer than it has to be.* She said, "Nothing for me, thanks."

Betsy plugged in her hot pot. She asked how we were liking Rogers, and who our favorite professors were. She was a nice girl from Syracuse, and you could tell that she took her job as resident adviser seriously.

She handed me the mug of soup; it was hot, and I blew on it.

She said, "You guys are spending an awful lot of time together." She was struggling. "You know, this is the time for making new friends," she said. "Meeting everybody."

We both said we'd made other friends, which was a little truer for me than for Venice.

Betsy said, "I just want to make sure you're open to other relationships."

I said, "I'm open."

Venice couldn't make herself say words like these, but she nodded and widened her eyes to convey openness.

Betsy said, "College is when you make the friendships that will last for the rest of your life." She looked miserable saying this.

She went from cliché to cliché, as though stepping from one flat stone to the next across a roiling river, until finally Venice said, "I think I understand what you're trying to say," though neither of us did.

A few days later we found out: There was a rumor that Venice and I were lesbians.

It didn't bother Venice at all, and I tried to act nonchalant, too. I asked if she wasn't afraid the rumor would prevent some hypothetical man from hypothetically falling in love with her.

She said the rumor wasn't going to prevent anyone from anything, just the opposite: According to Georges, ninety percent of men had lesbian fantasies.

I said, "But what if he's in the other ten percent?"

She said, "The other ten percent are gay."

Then Venice met Hugh, and that was that.

· · · · ·

Technically, Hugh wasn't as handsome as Venice was beautiful. He had dark hair and always a few days' worth of dark beard. His skin was bad—red and rough and maybe damaged from acne; there were scars. Yet this seemed to make him more attractive, as it never would a woman. Like Venice, though, Hugh was admired from afar, and he affected women as strongly as she did men, and maybe more deeply—not that he had any idea.

He lived off campus, in a dingy apartment with worn-out uphol-stered chairs and an olive vinyl sofa, but leaning against the walls were his own beautiful landscape paintings. The apartment had an unheated sunporch facing the lake, and Venice said he'd bundle up and paint out there, wearing his winter coat and gloves he'd cut the fingers off of.

The two of them were always inviting people over to his apart-ment before and after parties. He always offered Pimm's—he'd been to London the year before and had brought back cases of it. If you wanted to drink something else, you brought it.

It was Venice who kept these evenings going. Hugh was no good at parties, even in his own home. He seemed older—much older—than his guests, almost grandfatherly. He reminded me of someone deaf, or nearly so; he had trouble keeping up with conversations, and con-tributed the non-est of non sequiturs. I once heard him interrupt a joke about Reagan to say that Millard Fillmore's birthplace was in nearby Locke, New York. He didn't seem to know how awkward he was, or if he did, didn't care; I don't think he cared what anyone except Venice thought of him. He trusted her opinions and sought them out; when she didn't like something he said, he wanted to know why—he was really eager to hear.

They didn't call each other Honey or Babe, let alone Flea or Cabbage; to each other they were Venice and Hugh. They hardly touched each other in front of other people. Their kisses hello or good-bye didn't say, *Sex*. But there was something private between them, enviably private. They were a couple in a way that didn't exclude anyone but seemed superior to every other relationship in the room.

· · · · ·

I never saw Venice get upset. Even after her worst fight with Hugh—he'd read an aerogram from Georges—Venice just said, "Hugh's being idiotic." So it was shocking and terrible one afternoon to find her crying in our room.

I didn't know what was wrong, and for a long time she was crying too hard to tell me. Finally, she got out enough words to let me know she'd gotten into Brown.

She hadn't told me she'd applied to transfer, and I wondered if she'd told Hugh. Not that it would matter; Hugh was graduating, anyway, and Brown was closer than Rogers to Manhattan, where he was looking for a job.

"You don't have to go," I said.

She gave me a look that reminded me of the first night when she'd wanted a drink and I'd told her about the soda machine.

Then more tears.

I told her I'd do anything if she would just stop crying, and right away she said, "Play your fiddle for me."

"Shit," I said, but I got it out of its case and looked through my records for one to play along with. The only songs I knew were the cowboy and miner ballads of the variety called High Lonesome, but I put on the happiest one I could think of—one about a cowboy's love for his horse.

I hadn't played for anyone in a long time, and I wasn't sure I could do it now. I had to stand with my back to her, which in itself was embarrassing.

When I stopped playing, Venice smiled—a huge relief, even though I wasn't sure if she was smiling with me or at me.

· · · · ·

That summer, Venice sent me a postcard a week from Europe. She'd seen Georges in Tuscany and described it in six languages, including pig Latin: *"Elt-fay othing-nay."*

In late August, she called from Capri to invite me to spend Labor Day weekend on Long Island, where Hugh's family had a house. I'd never gotten a call from Europe and wasn't sure how expensive it was, and I found myself saying yes because it was faster than saying no, which would have required an explanation.

Hugh and Venice picked me up at the train, in his grandparents' old station wagon. Venice gave me the front seat, and I looked out at the bushes of blue hydrangeas, the huge shade trees, and the houses with their silvered cedar shingles.

Hugh's was on the bay side, across Dune Road from the beach. The house was big but shabby; his family had managed to hold on to the house but had no money to keep it up. You'd open a drawer and the pull would come off in your hand.

I was worried that I'd feel awkward as the guest of Venice, as a guest of a guest, a guest once-removed. But Hugh introduced me to his mother and grandparents and sister as his "great friend," and that was how I felt.

· · · · ·

My favorite time of day was the late, late afternoon with the sun golding up the ocean and sand and sea grass and dunes. Venice said it was called "magic hour" in the movies. She knew because she'd read a few scripts by then, given to her by a director she'd met that summer.

One magic hour, after swimming, we got dressed on the beach in jeans and sweaters. We unpacked a dinner picnic of leftovers—cold crabs and cold corn on the cob and tomatoes Venice had flecked with fresh basil. Hugh made a fire, and we drank wine and stayed out there on the beach late into the night.

When we got back everyone was asleep, and Venice went off to Hugh's bedroom, as she did every night. She'd come back to ours just as the sky was getting light, and sometimes I'd wake up and remember where I was and I'd feel as happy then as I ever had.

· · · · ·

The three of us were happy as quahogs until Labor Day. It was overcast, and I thought that was what made the morning seem slow and thick.

Without much enthusiasm, Hugh suggested sailing.

Venice looked dubious; she noted the lack of wind. Then she said, "Our train leaves at four."

Hugh said, "I know what time your train leaves."

Venice seemed oblivious to his tone, and maybe she was at first. However upset she'd been when she'd gotten into Brown, I knew she was excited now about going. She wasn't talking about it, but she radiated the exuberance you can feel about going to a new place or starting a new thing.

Hugh wasn't going anywhere or starting anything; he hadn't found a job yet.

Finally we went sailing, without any of us really wanting to. It was a little boat, not much bigger than a Sunfish, and it looked old. As I got in, I asked Hugh when it had last been used.

Hugh seemed to wonder himself for a minute, and I thought, *Three drown in boating accident.*

Both Venice and Hugh knew how to sail, and all I really did was watch them and the bay, lower my head when the boom crossed over, and look forward to going back to the house and taking one last outdoor shower before getting on the train.

The sky clouded over, and there was no sun at all anymore, and no wind, either. Finally Venice said, "We should head back." Hugh didn't answer, just turned the boat around.

They had to tack—zigzag—the whole way back across the bay. Hugh kept sighing, and he seemed annoyed. He was giving Venice orders, like, "Just get over there," and she was obeying them. She didn't seem angry or upset or embarrassed, as I would have been. I thought maybe the windlessness was more dire than I realized, and the two of them were following emergency sailing procedures, which included the captain acting like a jerk and his mate ignoring him.

But neither changed, even once we got close to shore and out of danger; again, I wondered if Venice was thinking less about where she was now than where she'd be later.

We were pulling the boat up onto the sand when I saw how wrong I was. Behind Hugh's back, her face was full of sympathy. Venice knew exactly what he was feeling: The life he'd known was about to end; it would end as soon as she got on the train. She knew that he was scared of losing her and scared of not finding a job, and this was her way of telling him he didn't have to be.

On the beach she did a cartwheel, and he did one, too, a failure, but she laughed and got him laughing.

Back at the house, Venice took the first shower. I was packing when Hugh came and stood in the doorway and said, "Why don't you stay another night?"

I told him that my older brother expected me to spend the night with him in Manhattan.

"Stay with me," he said, and his look let me know I would be doing him a favor.

· · · · ·

At a restaurant on Main Street, Hugh and I sat outside, drinking scotch for dinner. We weren't talking at all. I felt awkward and tried to think up topics other than the girlfriend who'd left and the job he didn't have.

When he recognized someone he knew and called him to the table, I was overjoyed.

Hugh rose and said, "Have a drink with us."

The guy tipped his head bar-ward and said, "I'm in the middle of something," and his tone said, *In the middle of some girl.* Then he said hi to me, and, "I'm Michael Whitmore," and I told him my name, and we shook hands. To Hugh, he said, "Call me at the office on Tuesday," and was gone.

Another year of silence passed before Hugh said, "I should've majored in economics."

It reminded me of how I'd felt applying to college. Night after night, I sat with my father in his study while he read aloud from *Barron's*. He'd read the name of the college, the number of men and the number of women, and a description in guidebook prose; then he'd say, "How does that sound?" and I'd think, *Sounds just like the last one.*

It took me a few nights to realize that my father was reading only the colleges that I had some chance of getting into—not Brown but Bowling Green; not Wesleyan but Ohio Wesleyan; not Williams or Smith, but William Smith. Until that moment, it hadn't occurred to me that my grades and test scores over the years were anything more than individual humiliations; I hadn't realized that one day all of them would add up and count against me.

My father was waiting to hear my reaction to whatever college he'd just read me the description of. He looked over at me. "What is it?"

"I wish someone had told me," I said.

"Told you what?"

I hadn't answered. I'd already figured out that not understanding my failings was another of my failings.

Now I wanted to convince Hugh that whatever prevented him from finding a job was not a failing but a strength. "You're a painter," I told him. "I don't even know why you're looking for a job in investment banking."

He said, "I need to make a living, Sophie."

"Maybe you could do something with art, though," I said.

He asked if I had any idea how much private-school tuition was.

"No." I waited for him to make his point. Then I realized he already had. He was talking about the cost of educating the children he planned to have with Venice.

I told Hugh that I didn't think Venice cared too much about money, but as I said it I realized I didn't know.

"She doesn't care about it," he said, "because she doesn't have to."

· · · · ·

I worried about Hugh, but there was no need: He got a job in Michael's bank, and ended up moving into Michael's apartment.

Venice didn't like Michael, and I was there the night Hugh asked her why. "Just tell me," he said. "I want to know."

She shrugged.

"Because I sleep in the living room?" Hugh said. "Is that it?"

"No."

He said, "It's his apartment."

Venice reminded Hugh that he paid half the rent.

He asked her once more what she had against Michael. When she wouldn't answer, he said, "Michael's a good friend of mine." His voice was serious, even stern.

She gazed at him—loving him, I think, for his loyalty to his friend—and then she said, "Okay."

· · · · ·

Venice spent almost every weekend in Manhattan, and the weekends I came in the three of us stayed at her parents' apartment, their pied-à-terre, on Seventy-ninth Street off Park. Friday afternoon, I'd take the bus down from Klondike, and Venice would take a train from Providence.

We'd meet near the apartment, at the Toy Bar. It was small and cozy, and you could ask the bartender for dominoes or checkers or practically any board game—Risk, Life, Operation, Parcheesi, Monopoly, even the Barbie Dating Game. There was a model train set, too, and a few times a night the bartender would press a switch and the train would clack and whistle around the track above our heads. The engine had a light on it.

We'd spend an hour or two there—Venice always made time for us to talk by ourselves—and then Hugh would join us. Sometimes she mentioned a party she knew of, though we rarely went; Hugh's awkwardness at parties had begun to bother Venice.

Hugh was obviously relieved to have a job, but I don't think he liked the actual work—selling bonds, I think; at least he never talked about it. When I asked him about his job, he'd say, "It's fine, fine," and his double fine made me think it was totally unfine. He was working hard, though. There were nights when he couldn't meet us until very late.

. . . . .

Thanksgiving break was the first time Venice mentioned Anthony. He was from England, and she pronounced his name not with a *th* but a *T* and a breath, as in *Antony and Cleopatra*.

We'd decided to walk all the way from her parents' apartment to Penn Station, where I would get the train home to Philadelphia and she'd meet Hugh for the one to Long Island.

Anthony was "incredibly smart," she said, and "incredibly charming," and "incredibly fun."

I said, "He sounds incredible."

She didn't compare him to Hugh directly, but she let me know that it was nice to be with someone who could hold his own at a cocktail party.

"Are you seeing him?" I said.

"God, no!" she said. "We just go to parties together."

I gave her a look: *Are you sure?*

She said, "He's a total lothario," and by then I felt comfortable enough with her to ask what a lothario was. "A seducer," she said. "A womanizer."

I had a bad feeling about him, but I didn't want to say so. What I said was, "Would I like him?"

"I think he'd intrigue you," she said. "But I'm not sure you'd like him."

We were in the Thirties on Fifth Avenue when someone handed us flyers for a sample sale, and Venice looked at hers. She said she'd heard of the designer and the showroom was on our way and, "Let's go."

Venice hated shopping, and I thought maybe she wanted to go to the sale to avoid more questions about Anthony.

On the elevator up, I said, "Does Hugh know?"

She said, "There's nothing to know."

Then we were in the frenzy of the sale, and Venice asked me to keep an eye out for a floor-length gown she needed for a formal party Anthony had invited her to—"a ball," she called it.

She found one, in cobalt silk, with a low, drapey back.

There were no dressing rooms—we had to try on our dresses in an aisle between racks—and no mirrors, either, so we had to rely on each other's judgment.

Venice said, "Don't be kind."

The cobalt dress looked fantastic on her, but I said so hesitantly; it occurred to me that if I could talk her out of the dress, maybe she wouldn't go to the ball with Anthony.

She didn't seem to hear me. She was staring at me and what I was wearing—a strapless black taffeta cocktail dress with a tight, boned bodice and a skirt that flounced and swirled to my knees.

Her voice was almost awed when she said, "Sophie." Then: "Take your bra off."

I looked at her, *Really?*

Her look said, *Obviously.*

I did as I was told, and she nodded.

I looked at the tag. "It's four hundred dollars."

She said, "These dresses go for thousands," and asked if I had enough in my checking account to cover it.

I said, "Are you kidding?"

She said, "Do you have a credit card?"

I did, but my father had given the card to me with specific instructions for its use—emergencies, and once a week I was to take myself and a friend out for a good dinner. I had, but never Venice; I'd been afraid she'd order a lot of drinks or an expensive bottle of wine, and then the big bill would go to my father, and he'd know I was turning out wrong.

I said, "I'm just supposed to use it for emergencies."

"This is an emergency."

I unzipped the dress.

She said, "Have I ever told you to buy anything before?"

We'd only shopped together once, at the Salvation Army thrift shop in Klondike, where she'd tried to talk me out of a sweater. "Of course it's not perfect," I'd said. "It's a dollar."

Now I said, "Name one place I could wear it."

She said, "I'm going to buy it for you if you won't."

I said, "Name one place."

She said that maybe I could go with her and Anthony to the ball. She thought for a minute. "You can wear it anywhere as long as you show up late. People will think you're coming from somewhere else, a gala or whatever."

I reminded her that I wasn't the kind of gal who went to galas.

"You don't understand," she said. "This is your one perfect thing."

When I told her it was just too expensive, she said that hers cost twice as much.

We were in line for the cashier before I thought of the ball she was going to with Anthony. For Hugh's sake, I said a doubtful, "Is yours a perfect thing, do you think?"

She said, "Perfect enough."

. . . . .

That night, at home in Surrey, in my childhood bedroom, I tried on the dress and looked in the mirror.

What I saw was so foreign to me that I couldn't take it in at first. In the dress, I was glamorous. I was elegant. I was a movie star, there in my bedroom with its canopy bed and Bob Dylan posters.

Venice was right: The dress was perfect, and it was perfect on me. The low-cut bodice accentuated my large breasts and made my waist appear tiny and my hips merely full. I wasn't used to seeing my bare shoulders, and especially not the flesh above my breasts, which even at a standstill called to mind the word *heaving*.

I looked at myself for a long while, and I remember it as one of the only times in my life when I saw myself as beautiful.

When my father knocked on my door, I told him that I was undressed, not a complete lie.

"Come say good night," he said.

I put on my nightgown and bathrobe and went into my parents' bedroom. I sat at the foot of their bed. My mother put down the old *New Yorker* she'd been reading.

"I have something to tell you," I said.

My mother looked worried, but my father, a judge, appeared as imperturbable as ever.

"I bought a dress," I said. "It was expensive."

"How expensive?" my mother said.

I couldn't make myself say the price out loud. I told my father that I would skip taking friends out to dinner for the rest of the year.

My father said, "You don't have to do that."

"Yes," I said, "I do."

My mother said, "How much was it, Sophie?"

I said, "It was on sale."

She kept her eyes on me. I said that it was by a famous designer, but then I couldn't remember who, and the label had been cut out of the dress.

Finally I told them the price.

Neither of my parents spoke.

I said what Venice had: The dress was worth thousands of dollars.

My father said, "And you feel you need a dress that's worth thousands of dollars?"

I didn't answer.

My parents took turns talking about my values. We all agreed that it was not appropriate or reasonable for me to buy a dress this expensive. We all agreed that I would return the dress. Then I remembered that my receipt was stamped FINAL SALE.

I said, "I'll pay you back."

My father nodded.

Then my mother said, "Do you love it?" which was what she said whenever we were shopping and I wanted to buy something expensive.

She'd say, "Do you really love it?" If I said yes, she'd go on to say that I could wear that expensive garment forever, for years and years, and all year round; whatever the fabric—sheerest cotton, heaviest wool—she'd proclaim it seasonless. She'd name places I could wear it, events in the near and distant future: I could wear it to a cousin's bar mitzvah, my brother's graduation, my own wedding, and I could be buried in it.

On the rare occasions when I could sustain the enthusiasm required for the purchase—there was always one final "Do you really love it?" at the register—at home the garment would hang in my closet like a cinder block around my neck.

Now my mother got in the spirit: "Try it on for us."

I said, "Tomorrow."

That winter, whenever I met Venice at the Toy Bar, she talked about Anthony; she seemed to need to—it was urgent. She talked fast so she could tell me everything before Hugh showed up.

She now admitted that Anthony was pursuing her. For her birthday, he'd taken her to Block Island, and driving to the ferry they'd passed a huge billboard that read HAPPY BIRTHDAY, ZSA ZSA.

She said, "He calls me Zsa Zsa."

"I got that," I said.

She heard the disapproval in my tone and said, "I've never even kissed him, Sophie."

. . . . .

One night, she told me that Anthony wanted to charter a plane to fly her to Maryland for soft-shell crabs.

I said, "Can't you get crabs in Providence?"

She looked at me.

"Are you falling in love with this guy?" I wanted to call him a lothario.

"No."

"So, what are you doing with him?"

I didn't like her at that moment, and I could tell that she didn't like me, either. I wondered, not for the first time, why we were friends.

She said, "We're not sleeping together, if that's what you're asking," and I heard the distance between that and "I've never even kissed him."

Hugh walked in then.

He seemed unsure of himself that night, and maybe that was why he'd brought Michael, a surprise to Venice, though she didn't show it, even when Michael kissed her cheek.

He sat down next to me and said, "We met in Quogue this summer."

I couldn't really talk because of what had just happened between Venice and me—and then because of what was happening between Venice and Hugh.

He was holding her hand, which I'd never seen him do before, and she seemed to be just barely allowing it. Once, she sort of snatched it away—she pretended it was to sip her drink—but the gesture stayed there in the air, and no one spoke for a long moment.

Michael said, "We need to play a game," and by "we" he meant he and I.

I assumed that he was just giving Venice and Hugh time alone. At the bar, though, he said, "What do you want to play?" and I heard something in there that had nothing to do with his friend or my friend or friendship.

"Checkers?" I said.

It was dark at the bar, but that wasn't the only reason I found it hard to see what Michael looked like. For one thing, his eyes were so deep-set there was a shadow across them. And he kept looking at me, and when I'd look over, he'd look away. I noticed his hair, though. It was straight and dark and longish, and I liked it.

I found myself drawn to him in a way I wasn't used to, and it was distracting. I kept losing at checkers. Every time he said, "King me," I stopped breathing.

He said, "Tell me your life story, Sophie Applebaum."

"You first," I said.

He made one up. He was a circus brat, he said. He told me that his father was a trapeze artist, and his mother, wearing a headdress and a spangled costume cut like a bathing suit, rode the tiger around the ring. After school, he fed the elephants, Floozy and Poco.

"Then the circus disbanded," he said. He shook his head. "It was really pretty sad."

His father couldn't find work and his mother became a chorus girl. He said her kicks had put him through Williams.

Another vodka tonic, and my knee touched his. When I moved it away, he said, "No," and I moved it back.

He was looking at me now, and not talking; neither of us was talking. I sent him an ESP message: *Touch me.* But he didn't, and I shocked and thrilled myself by reaching under the bar for his hand.

He was looking at me more intently than I'd ever been looked at, and I saw in his eyes that he needed me and wanted me, and I felt that I'd never needed and wanted anyone so much, and probably never would again.

What I thought was: *We are falling in love.*

"I'm a little tired, Sophie Applebaum," he said. He looked at me. "I think I'm going to head home."

I knew what he was asking, and it reminded me of a scene Venice had read to me from *Anna Karenina,* when Kitty and Levin are playing a parlor game of initials and they telepathically know the words the initials stand for. I thought, *We are telepathic; we are Kitty and Levin.*

Just then the model train went around the track, and we both looked up.

We walked over to where Venice and Hugh sat.

"I'm going to head out," Michael said, and I said, "Me, too."

Venice looked up at me, and I saw an expression I hadn't seen before—concern, I thought, or even worry. I assumed it was because of our bad crab moment, so I leaned down and, with all the affection I had for her, said, "I'll talk to you tomorrow."

"Are you sure?" she asked.

"Yes," I said.

Michael said, "See you Monday," to Hugh.

Then we were outside, on the curb.

Michael said, "Are you sure you want to do this?"

I said, "I'm sure."

"I'll want to see you anyway," he said, "whether you come with me now or not."

To be fair, it was the only real lie he told.

I cringe even now, remembering my response: "I know that."

. . . . .

For weeks, every time the hall phone rang it wasn't Michael; every letter in my mailbox wasn't from him.

Venice never brought him up. When I'd ask if she'd seen him, she'd sigh and say she had. I knew it was wrong to blame her, but I did a little. When I tried to name how she was responsible or what she'd done wrong, all I could come up with was that it wouldn't have happened to her.

I thought about *The Heiress*, and what I'd do if Michael did finally knock on my door. I knew what Venice would say; if you thought about it, though, "Bar the door, Maria" was what Catherine says on her way upstairs to spend the rest of her life alone.

I didn't know what I'd say. I hoped that Michael's excuse would be so good, his apology so enormous, his gesture of reconciliation so *Happy Birthday, Zsa Zsa* that I wouldn't need to say anything.

. . . . .

I still met Venice at the Toy Bar, and she still talked about Anthony, though not as much. She tried to act like he was slowing down and possibly giving up and that she didn't care either way. She spoke in the calm, even voice people use in an accelerating emergency.

It was harder for me to see Hugh now because of what I knew about Anthony. I felt like I was lying, even when I was just saying hello. Hugh must have sensed what was going on, though—he seemed less and less sure of himself.

. . . . .

"I have to tell you something," Venice said to me one night at the Toy Bar. "Before Hugh gets here."

I already knew that she was sleeping with Anthony, but I didn't want to hear it. Once she said the words out loud, everything would change. I shook my head: *Please don't tell me.*

I could see that she didn't want to. She steeled herself. Then she forced the words out: "Michael won't stop calling me." Her voice was a little shaky as she told me; she knew the risk she was taking.

She was trying to be a good friend, and I appreciated that, in theory.

"Don't tell Hugh, please," she said. "He has few enough friends as it is."

. . . . .

Hugh had more friends than Venice did, though—or fewer enemies.

We never found out who'd seen her with Anthony that weekend in Manhattan, the weekend she'd told Hugh she needed to stay in Providence to write a paper.

She kept going over every public moment of that weekend, trying to identify the one that had cost her Hugh. She'd helped Anthony choose a tie at Barneys; they'd spiraled up and down the Guggenheim; they'd gone to the Carlyle to hear Bobby Short. She said she hadn't seen anyone see her, not anyone she knew, and it occurred to me that she wouldn't have noticed anyone's gaze, she was so used to being looked at.

. . . . .

I avoided meeting Anthony until the following winter.

Venice didn't hear the dread in my voice. She told me to bring my perfect dress and she'd bring her cobalt—Anthony would figure out somewhere good for us to go—and I carried the dress in a garbage bag on the bus down.

I stowed it with my duffel bag under the table at the Toy Bar and waited for Venice.

She was late and walked in apologizing. She said that Anthony would be here any minute; they'd fought, she said, and he needed to cool off. She couldn't talk about their argument because he might walk in, and she couldn't talk about anything else.

She looked as beautiful as I'd ever seen her, but different. I saw that she was wearing makeup, and I was so surprised that I said it out loud.

She said, "Anthony likes to make me up."

"He puts makeup on you?"

She nodded.

"He's good," I said.

She said, "He's sort of an artist."

I said, "Maybe he could make me up sometime."

She either didn't like the joke or didn't hear it; she was nervous. She kept looking at her watch and taking her bangle bracelet off and putting it back on.

When some guy came over to the table, she surprised me by inviting him to sit down. He was no more captivating than any of the men I'd seen her dismiss over the years, but she kept talking to him, and she let him buy our drinks. He was still there when Anthony walked in, and it occurred to me that she'd staged this.

Anthony was very tall and conventionally handsome, and there was something flashy about him, or flashing—his eyes flashed; he flashed a smile. Later, whenever Venice talked about him, I pictured him in a Dracula cape.

He didn't sit down. He looked around the Toy Bar, and he didn't like it. He said, "I thought we might go to the Algonquin," and Venice stood, though we hadn't finished our drinks.

I got my bags from under the table, and Anthony took them from me.

"Nice luggage," he said, giving my garbage bag a twist. "I have the same set at home." I thought I might like him.

In the cab, he and Venice talked about the Algonquin Round Table and repeated the witty remarks they knew. When we got out of the cab, he held his garbage-bag arm out for her and said, "Mrs. Parker," and she took it and said, "Thank you, Mr. Benchley."

Inside, though, it was just a hotel bar, and it felt like no one had said anything witty there in a long time.

"Maybe we should get a round table," Venice said, but Anthony said we were better off where we were. Venice moved a stool aside and stood, and Anthony sat between us. He alternated between holding her waist and his drink.

"So," he said, "you're the famous Sophie from Roger."

"Rogers," I said.

He said, "Sorry?" using the word but not the intonation of apology.

"It's called Rogers."

"Right." He said a sorrier, "Sorry."

Anthony seemed restless. The whole time we were there he talked about where else we could go: He'd been invited to a party uptown, or maybe we should go to Studio 54; there was a great after-hours club he knew of, but, he said, it might be early for that.

"You know what?" I said. "I'm tired."

Venice looked worried. When I said that I was going to stay at my brother's, she didn't argue.

We were saying good-bye when she smiled at me, and I knew what she was about to do; in a sexed-up voice, she said, "Do you mind if I sleep with your husband?"

Maybe she wanted to restore something between us, but it seemed more like a performance for Anthony—*My Funny Friendship with Sophie*—and it didn't come off. She was still explaining the joke to him when I left.

. . . . .

"I'm sorry Anthony was so rude," she said on the phone the next morning.

Anthony had seemed cold, arrogant, bored, and capable of cruelty, but not rude. What I'd mainly noticed was how nervous she'd been.

"He felt threatened," she said.

I thought maybe I'd misheard her, and I said what Anthony would have: "Sorry?"

"Because of Hugh," she said. "Because you're a friend of Hugh's."

I didn't know what to say; I hadn't talked to Hugh since before they'd broken up. He hadn't returned my calls.

Venice was saying, "He's insanely jealous of Hugh," and I thought I heard a trace of an English accent in her voice. "Anyway," she said, "we'll go out tonight, and you can wear the dress."

Suddenly, I missed Hugh.

"Anthony wants to take us to some party in SoHo," she said. "We'll go really late."

I didn't answer right away. It occurred to me to make up an excuse, but then I said, "I don't want to."

She was quiet, and I was, too.

I couldn't really believe that she'd decided to be with Anthony, whom I would never choose over Hugh, or choose over anyone, or choose over no one. That made it hard for me to believe that Venice and I were the same person underneath everything, which was what I thought love required.

. . . . .

I wore the perfect dress three times.

In my senior year at Rogers, I wore the dress to a fraternity formal, and it was thrilling to be approached by men who'd never noticed me, and thrilling to be swarmed. I thought, *This is what it's like to be Venice,* and at first I liked it; I loved it. But it was tiring, too, and also I didn't like my date as much as he liked me, and it seemed wrong to wear a dress that might make him like me more.

The second time was to a Halloween party at my brother's girlfriend's apartment. I wore the dress with a deer mask. On the elevator up to the party, a tiny pirate said, "Who is she, Mommy?" and when Mommy asked me, I told her I was Bambi, Rudolph's mistress.

She looked down at her son and said, "She's Bambi, Rudolph's sister."

The last time I wore the dress was to a party Venice asked me to. It was one of those parties people gave then, men mostly; they'd rent a restaurant and invite people off of lists. You had to pay to get in. Her idea was that we go very late, and wear our dresses.

I'd been working in New York for a year by then, and Venice had, too. She had a small part in a soap opera. We'd hardly seen each other. When I'd ask her about Anthony, she wouldn't say much. She wanted to know when she was going to meet my new boyfriend. I said that Josh was pretty busy writing poetry.

The party was on East Sixth Street, at an Indian restaurant decorated with magenta velvet ottomans and gold drapes. Everyone else was wearing work clothes; the men who approached me asked where

I'd just come from. I stayed there for about an hour, waiting for Venice to show.

．．．．．

Maybe because she felt bad about standing me up, Venice told me about Anthony as she never had before. They'd had a horrible fight, she said, maybe their worst, though she added that the competition for this title was stiff. She told me how insane Anthony was and that he called her horrible names and was always accusing her of sleeping with other men, or wanting to.

When she said that she knew she had to leave him, I said, "You absolutely do."

She said, "I know," but there was no resolve in her voice.

She did finally leave him, though; she found out he'd been pursuing another woman all along.

．．．．．

I wasn't sorry that I went to the party.

Michael looked pretty much the same, though it had been dark outside the restaurant in Quogue and in the Toy Bar, and especially dark in his bedroom. The Indian restaurant was brightly lit.

I saw him out of the corner of my eye, and for the first time that night I was glad to be wearing my perfect dress.

I'd envisioned this moment many times: I'd pictured turning my back to him or slapping his face or pretending that I couldn't quite place him, I'd had so many lovers since him, my first, and all of them so much more memorable.

But when our eyes met and his look asked if I remembered him, my look answered that I did.

He came up to me as I was leaving. He asked if I wanted to go somewhere else for a drink, and I said that I couldn't.

How was Hugh? I asked. He was fine. Was he painting? He did paint sometimes.

Michael walked me outside, and we stood talking on the sidewalk— or he talked. I was pretty sure I wouldn't fall under his spell again, but to be safe I kept my eyes on his nose.

He was talking fast—he had a girlfriend but she was in Prague—

and anyway they were breaking up—they'd practically already broken up—and I nodded while he talked, the way you do when you're waiting for someone to finish.

"Well," I said, "I have to go."

He said, "Can I call you?"

I waited a long time before answering, though not, of course, as long as he'd made me wait. I let him stand there with the question in the air while I took a good long look at him, let him stand there while I stepped to the street and raised my arm for a cab. At exactly that moment, as though dispatched by some god I didn't really believe in anymore—the god of drama or god of perfect things—or maybe by my own fairy god god, a cab came. I got in, and closed the door.

20TH-CENTURY TYPING

1.

New York gave me a feeling of possibility I'd never gotten in the suburbs, driving home from Lord & Taylor with my mother, say. There, when I'd see people in other cars, I'd know they were on their way home, where their choices would be the same as mine: They could watch TV or read. In New York that summer, especially at dusk, in the Village or in midtown or on the Upper West Side, walking in a crowd of people or looking up at all the lit windows of an office or apartment building, I could feel like there were a thousand ways my life could go.

I'd just graduated from college and was teaching myself how to type at my brother Robert's apartment, a prewar dust factory on 119th Street and Broadway, just a few steps from a bank of pay phones that served as an alfresco urinal.

"Pissoir," my older brother called it, when he came for dinner; Jack lived by himself in a beautiful one-bedroom in the historic West Village.

Robert had three roommates, including his girlfriend, Naomi, who was quiet and serious. She was an unusually slow speaker, and I thought this might have something to do with her being Orthodox. I wondered if this strictest form of Judaism also dictated her sometimes wearing a bandanna over her long, wavy hair, which made her look like a girl from the shtetl in *Fiddler on the Roof.*

That summer, Naomi was applying to doctoral programs in psychology and Robert was studying for his MCAT; they lived in the library at Columbia and slept in her bedroom. It was the brightest room, but it faced the street and could be loud. Salsa music came in and fought the Mozart on her stereo. I lived in Robert's room, where I attended my own private secretarial school.

The apartment was big but dingy and full of cockroaches no one but me seemed to notice. It was especially depressing during the day when the sun shone through the dirty windows and let you know just how dirty everything was and always had been and always would be.

I was told that there were separate dishes for meat and milk, but I kept forgetting which was for which. One morning, when I was eating breakfast, Naomi came in and her mouth opened in what looked like a shriek. Instead, one of her ultra-white hands went up to her black hair, as though to calm her crazy self down.

"What?" I said.

I'd been eating my cereal out of a meat bowl.

When I offered to wash it out, she just stared at me.

I said, "What about if I use really, really hot water?"

She said the bowl would have to be thrown away, which seemed a little extreme, but as the criminal I wasn't in a position to choose the bowl's punishment.

. . . . .

She got Robert to talk to me about what I'd done, which I didn't think boded well for her future as a psychologist.

That evening the two of them came through the front door together, but Naomi took a left to her bedroom and Robert a right to the living room, where I sat with his roommate Leah.

He said hello to both of us and went to the kitchen and mixed his evening cocktail, a cranberry juice and seltzer.

He leaned in the doorway, sipping it, while Leah told me about the teaching fellowship she'd start in the fall in Tel Aviv. Her words were boring to me, but her voice, a soft monotone, was so soothing I kept asking her questions so she'd go on: "What does Tel Aviv look like?" "How do Israeli universities differ from the ones here?"

Robert stood there, waiting for Leah to finish, and when it looked to him like that might never happen, he motioned with his head for me to join him in his room.

I did, and he closed the door. I sat on the bed he never slept in, and I wondered about that: It seemed unlikely that the Orthodox leaders who shook their long curls at the cereal in my meat bowl would say, "Fine, fine," to premarital sex.

I tried to pay attention while Robert explained that Naomi's strict observance of rituals stemmed from deep religious beliefs. I came to life when he started talking about our family. In Naomi's eyes we were about as Jewish as Episcopalians. She'd been horrified that we'd had Christmas trees when we were growing up, and, as he told me, I remembered Robert as a little boy, dumping out his stocking of chocolate coins and matchbox cars, and his glee, in contrast to his current gloom.

I tried to cheer him up with a joke about the meatlike cockroaches illicitly lounging on milk plates in the cabinet, but he looked hurt, and when he said, "Sophie," a reprimand, I got a sick feeling. He'd been going with Naomi to synagogue some Friday nights and Saturday mornings; I'd assumed Robert was just being Robert, i.e., a good egg, but now I worried that maybe he was on the way to becoming a Torah-thumper himself.

He said, "We opened our home to you," which I knew was a direct quote from Naomi.

I said, "Did you just say, 'We opened our home to you'?"

His face registered that I'd busted him, and for a second his face belonged to the Robert I knew. Then we heard Naomi go down the hall for her shower, and he fixed his face back to dead seriousness.

I told him I'd apologize to her.

He said, "I think that's a good idea."

I asked if I needed to apologize to the other roommates, Leah and Seth, and he said no, Naomi was the only one who kept kosher. He seemed to think it was normal for one person to dictate the dietary laws for five.

In the kitchen, he pointed out which dishes were for what. As it turned out, there was a separate set of milk silverware I hadn't even known about, as well as separate pots and pans. He found a Magic

Marker and wrote out labels on masking tape and stuck them on the shelves and drawers. We both acted like, *Problem solved.*

. . . . .

After Robert left to go back to the library, I went down the hall to Naomi's room. The door was open; she was sitting at her desk writing a paper that might have been on conflict avoidance. Her hair hung thick and wet on a towel she'd draped over her bathrobe. It occurred to me that her hair would take all night to dry and that she'd sleep with a towel on her pillow, as I had when I was little. This made me think of her as young and clean instead of strict, which was the word that stuck in my mind from Robert's speech about her religious observance.

Strict came back, though, in her expression, when I knocked on the door frame and she turned around. She seemed to know that she was not only right in this specific instance, but generally right, righteously right, and I pictured her acting like this with Robert.

I was standing up for him and for my entire assimilated family and even the Christmas trees of my childhood, which I myself found strange, when I said, "Sorry about the cereal," as in, *Let's not forget we're talking about Cheerios here.*

. . . . .

I was just starting to go out with Robert's MCAT tutor, whom my genius brother called a genius.

Josh was gentle and polite, a poet and a lover of classic novels and foreign movies. He didn't drink and had never tried a single drug, and even during the Hades days of July, as he called them, he gave the impression of having just showered; he smelled faintly of baby powder.

He had long hair, which he pulled back in a ponytail, and he was lanky without actually being tall. Robert told me Josh was a great tennis player, and one night I went to the courts to see the two of them play. I loved watching Josh—especially his huge, powerful serve; he had beautiful form.

Afterward, walking home, I said, "You should see me type sometime."

. . . . .

Along with my father's huge IBM Selectric II, I'd brought a book called *20th-Century Typewriting* that I'd checked out from the library during my brief stint of postgraduation paralysis at home in the suburbs. A faded olive hardback, bound at the top like a pad, this was the book I'd used in junior-high typing class. I'd hoped some of the lessons would come back, but they hadn't.

On breaks from typing, I studied the résumé book I'd bought, *Advertisements for Yourself,* though even its encouragement discouraged me. These job-seekers had spent their entire lives preparing for the jobs I only now realized I might want. Tim J. Sullivan had been a journalism major, the editor of the campus newspaper, and a summer intern at a Detroit metropolitan daily with a circulation of twenty thousand. Laura Johnson, whose goal it was to assist a photographer, had already assisted one, worked in a gallery, and received an honorable mention in a juried exhibit at the Minnesota State Fair.

Only Lisa Michele Butler was of any use to me. Though I hadn't written a prizewinning thesis entitled "Regionalism in the Short Stories of Sarah Orne Jewett" or spearheaded a volunteer-based literacy initiative, I had been an English major. Therefore, like Lisa Michele, I sought an entry-level position in book publishing, preferably as an editorial assistant.

· · · · ·

Following the book's advice, I had my résumé typeset and was stunned by the effect: In plain, beautiful type, my lack of experience, accomplishments, and honors came across as understatement and modesty. I loved how my résumé looked so much that I forgot my fear about its content and showed it to Josh.

He said, "I don't know what you've been so worried about."

I said that he should see the résumés in *Advertisements for Yourself.*

"Honey," he said, "those aren't real people."

I said, "I know that. Now."

· · · · ·

I called the first person on Jack's list of people he knew in publishing, but either Jack got the name wrong or his friend had left the company; I was transferred to personnel.

I explained that I was looking for a friend of my brother's. "I'm sorry," I said.

The woman said, "Take your time."

I managed to say that I was looking for a job as an editorial assistant, and the woman, apparently a saint, asked if I could come into the office that afternoon.

I put on my seersucker suit and panty hose and pumps, which blistered my feet after only a few blocks.

The personnel saint was even nicer in person. She nodded at my résumé and smiled even when she told me that she'd never heard of the college I'd graduated from.

I told her not to worry: No one had heard of Rogers. "My brother calls it Hammerstein," I said.

"Fine," she said. "Can you type?"

I heard this as, *Are you willing?* and I said, "Absolutely."

Then she gave me the test.

After calculating my score, she said, "I'm sorry," and explained that I needed at least forty-five words per minute to be considered for any entry-level position in publishing.

I said, "How did I do?"

"Nine," she said.

· · · · ·

That night, instead of seeing Josh, I typed. I was restless, though, and kept going into the kitchen for a diet Coke or another coffee. Each time, Naomi appeared. She'd get herself a glass of water or look in the refrigerator, but I knew she was just in there to make sure I used the right dishes and silverware. I smiled at her: *But you don't know which I use when you're not around, do you?*

· · · · ·

Josh liked to stay in New York on weekends. He liked how the city emptied out, and you could go to museums or eat in restaurants that were usually crowded. I understood that, but my parents had a house on the New Jersey shore, and I wanted to go there sometimes. I wanted to swim in the ocean.

I said this to Josh one Friday night in August, when the humidity made me feel desperate and shrill.

Josh said, "We've already been there twice." He said, as he had before, that he wanted us to have new experiences together.

We began to have one right then, when he suggested we go to Coney Island to visit his Russian grandmother, Bubbe, who, on our first meeting, asked why I hadn't come to see her sooner.

I kept my voice even. "We've already been there," I said.

"Oh," he said. "Right."

Irrelevantly, I added that I hadn't seen my own grandmother even once.

Josh said, "Didn't I just meet her?"

He'd met my mother's mother, Steeny, at the shore. "I'm talking about my father's mother, Grandma Mamie," I said. "She lives in the Bronx."

"Well," he said, as though we had a wonderful solution right in front of us, "let's visit her."

I said that the last thing I wanted do on a summer day was see anybody's grandmother. "Don't you understand?" I felt like I must not be speaking clearly, and I tried to find the right words. "I need to get out," I said, and even to myself I sounded like a child throwing a tantrum over something like a drop of coleslaw touching my hamburger.

"You want to take a walk?" he said.

I shook my head. My frustration was escalating, a headache coming on.

He said, "Why don't you stand by the fan?"

Josh became eerily calm; he was the eye of the storm, and I became its mouth. Finally, I took my ranting self out of there and walked up Broadway to Robert's.

When I got there, I couldn't find my keys. I buzzed the intercom and waited; I buzzed again. When I stood back and looked up, I saw a light on in Naomi's bedroom—or rather, candles lit, and I remembered that it was the Sabbath.

I called from one of the pissoir phones. The answering machine picked up, and Leah's recorded "shalom" calmed me down. After the beep, I said, "It's Sophie," and, "I'm locked out."

I waited, and the voice-activated machine hung up on me.

I was pretty sure the library closed at ten o'clock on Friday nights. It was 10:10 now. I figured that Robert would come home soon. I sat on the stoop and waited.

But then a terrible thought occurred to me: What if Robert was upstairs? I couldn't picture him refusing to let me in, no matter what Naomi said. But she ruled the kitchen, and the front door was just down the hall.

Finally, a delivery man was buzzed into the building, and I followed him inside. Upstairs I knocked on the door, and a few minutes later Naomi answered in her bathrobe. She said, "I was asleep," which came out as a statement of fact, but if it listed anywhere it was closer to reprimand than apology.

I got into bed and lay there, listening for Robert. A few minutes later he unlocked the front door. He went down the hallway to Naomi's room without turning on a single light.

· · · · ·

When I woke up, Robert and Naomi had already gone, probably to her synagogue.

There were two messages from Josh on the answering machine. The first—"It's Josh . . . I have Sophie's keys"—was so cold and matter-of-fact it made me feel we'd already broken up. The second—"Please call me"—was so sad and intimate he might have been whispering in my ear.

He was sorry; I was sorry; we were sorry. We spent all Saturday making up in his apartment.

· · · · ·

On Sunday, Robert said, "I'm sorry about Friday night."

I said, "It's not your fault."

Without mentioning Naomi, he defended her: He explained what couldn't be done on the Sabbath and why.

I waited until he'd finished. Then I said, "Are you Orthodox now, Robert?"

He shook his head but told me he liked observing the Sabbath—"It's nice and quiet"—and reminded me that he'd always liked going to synagogue. "What's not to like?" he said. "It's a roomful of Jews."

Later, Naomi knocked on my door, and when I turned around, I realized that she was standing just as I had when I'd gone to her room to apologize.

She said, "Sorry about the buzzer."

·　·　·　·　·

She went off to the library, and Robert and I had dinner with his roommates. Leah was leaving for Tel Aviv in just a few weeks, and Seth said that they had to start looking for another roommate now. "What about you, Soph?" Seth said. "Don't you need an apartment?"

Leah's eyes widened, and I realized that Naomi had talked to her about me.

Robert had stopped eating. He was looking down at his plate, and when he looked up at me, his face was helpless. On it, I could see that a yes to me would mean a no to Naomi. I didn't want him to feel that it was Girlfriend vs. Sister, but I knew he would no matter what.

I made my face say, *It's okay.*

I told the table that I needed to find a job before I rented an apartment.

·　·　·　·　·

I could see that Robert was relieved when I told him that I was going to stay with Jack for a while.

It was awkward when I moved out. I stood with Naomi and Robert by the door for a few minutes, saying good-bye. Josh had carried my stuff downstairs, where Jack was waiting for me in his convertible. I had all my clothes on hangers draped over my arm when Robert tried to hug me.

"Well," I said, and then, accidentally: "Thank you for opening your home to me."

2.

JACK CALLED NAOMI "Gnomie" and "The Gnomester," and he laughed at my cockroach joke. When I repeated Robert's "We opened our home" remark, Jack shook his head and said, "Robby, Robby, Robby."

It was my first night in Jack's apartment, and we had just finished a great dinner that his girlfriend, Cynthia, had cooked. She'd put tulips on the table, and the kitchen was dark except for candles. It was a nice atmosphere, and I was glad to be there, but I also felt bad about the way the conversation was going.

Jack said, "There's a word for what our little brother has become."

I said, "I don't know about that."

He said, "Oh, I think you do."

He was talking to me, but he was also teasing Cynthia, who was from Alabama and probably didn't cotton to words like *pussy-whipped*.

"Jack," I said, "I think he's going to marry her," and I realized it was true. Now that I thought about it, they acted like they were already married.

I wondered how Jack would feel about his little brother getting married before him. Maybe Cynthia wondered, too; she was looking at him.

He was quiet, and I could tell he was picturing the talk he might have with Robert; he even moved his lips a little. Whatever he imagined, I was pretty sure Robert wouldn't listen. Jack knew how to make women fall in love with him, but that didn't exactly qualify him as a guidance counselor.

When Jack came out of his reverie, he asked how my job hunt was going and whether I'd met any of the editors whose numbers he'd given me. He didn't mention their names in front of Cynthia, and it occurred to me that they were all women he'd gone out with.

I said that I was waiting until I could type forty-five words per minute.

Cynthia gave me a big, encouraging smile. *You'll get there, Sugar Bear.*

She was tall with very long arms and a big, red-lipsticked mouth. She was a clothing designer and had one of those personalities that drapes itself all over you at first. She'd hugged me when we'd met, for example, and talk-talk-talked all through dinner, not that I minded. She had a pretty voice and in it you could hear the song of the South at the end of a sentence.

We stayed up a long time talking, and I did the dishes. Afterward, when I went out to the living room, Cynthia was tucking sheets and a blanket into the futon sofa I'd sleep on.

Jack opened his bedroom door just enough for his head, so I knew he was in his underwear or nothing; he said, "Good night, Tinkerbell."

Cynthia gave me a little squeeze. "I'm glad you're here," she said, which made me love her.

· · · · ·

I'd never heard anyone having sex before, and it took a few minutes for me to realize that's what it was. Faintly, I heard Cynthia whimpering. Jack sounded the way he had lifting weights in our basement, sort of a growl that got louder and in the past had ended with the crash of barbells. Then they were both laughing, and I kind of laughed, too.

Josh and I were silent when we had sex, and I thought the next time I would make some noise.

I didn't, though. The next night at dinner, Josh told me that he needed to spend more time writing poetry.

We were at Szechwan West—Szech West, we called it—around the corner from his apartment; we'd just ordered.

Before meeting me, he explained, he'd spent every night writing in the library; now, he said, he was just going to his day job and seeing me at night. He said, "My poetry is really suffering."

I smiled when I said, "I don't want your poetry to suffer."

I tried to keep the conversation on poetry, instead of asking, say, whether he'd fallen out of love with me. But "What are your poems like?" dead-ended into him saying that he'd show them to me; "Who are your favorite poets?" resulted in a list.

When he asked who mine were, I sighed, as though musing among many, and tried to think of one. Finally, I recited my favorite poem:

> Shake and shake
> the ketchup bottle
> none'll come and
> then a lot'll.

Our dishes arrived, and he warned me about the hot peppers in mine. He said, "I ate one of those once, and it made me want to blow my head off."

At his apartment, in his bedroom, it was harder to pretend that everything was okay. I told him I was going to smoke a cigarette, which meant going outside the apartment. One of his roommates smoked, but just in her bedroom; Josh complained about the fumes that came out when she opened her door.

I felt better as soon as I was out in the stairwell. I sat on the dusty black steps and lit a cigarette. I sat there and tried to get my personality back.

Back inside, I opened the door to Josh's bedroom. He'd already turned out the light. I inched forward in the dark. My knee found the bed, and I got in. I lay very still. Then Josh put his arms around me, and it was safe to love him again.

· · · · ·

Every time I called home, my mother told me she'd received another overdue notice for *20th-Century Typewriting*.

Its main author was D. D. Lessenberry, and those Ds might have stood for Deadly, Dull, Dread, or Doom. All day, D. D. bored me with exercises and drills called "Know Your Typewriter" and "Reach Stroke Review," for which I typed such paragraphs as

Do you think you can learn to type well? It is up to you, you know. You build the right kind of skill through the way you work and the way you think; so think right and type right and you will have this prize of fine skill.

Around 6:30, Cynthia came through the door, with groceries for dinner and clothes in dry cleaner's plastic; she had her own apartment and supposedly wasn't living with Jack. She carried her groceries in a string bag that bulged with big and little brown bags. Instead of shopping at the supermarket around the corner on Bleecker Street, she went to the fish store or the butcher, to the cheese shop and bakery and the farmers' market. She said this was how people shopped in Paris, where she'd lived after art school.

She'd ask how my day was, and I'd say, "Okay," or, "All right." I wanted to say more, but a day of typing did not produce fascinating anecdotes. What could I say? *Well, Cynthia, I'm finally settling into the home keys.*

When Jack came through the door, I turned off the typewriter and carried it from the kitchen into the living room; I stowed it under the coffee table.

He'd say, "What's the score?" meaning how many words per minute, and I'd tell him the miserable number. Sometimes he called me Katie, which I didn't get; Katie, one of my best friends from college, had been a diligent student, but did he know that? When I finally asked him, he explained that Katie was short for Katharine Gibbs, the secretarial school.

Cynthia called Jack "Big Old Bear," which she pronounced *bar* and said in the voice of a little girl with a cold. It was apt: Jack was big and meaty and covered with fur everywhere but his head. She said it with great affection, and usually he'd take her in his big beary arms and maybe kiss her.

The living room was small, just the futon sofa and a few chairs that you were supposed to look at rather than sit in. But the kitchen was big and airy and looked out on leafy trees turning yellow and red, and that's where we all hung out.

While Cynthia cooked, Jack read the newspaper, and I'd read a section, too, even though I was dying to talk and be talked to. I'd make myself be quiet, though, and that felt nice after a while.

Sitting down for dinner, I could feel that we were a small, happy family.

After I'd done the dishes, I'd meet a friend for a drink or go up to Josh's. If I didn't have plans, I'd take a walk around the neighborhood to give Cynthia and Jack privacy. I'd walk up Christopher Street, which was still the center of gay life then. When I saw men kiss I didn't believe it at first.

. . . . .

Finally, I reached twenty-five words per minute, where I peaked and plateaued.

I told Jack this when he came through the door. "I'll be an old lady and typing twenty-five," I said, and I made my voice creaky and said, "Still twenty-five."

He laughed, but the next night when he came home, and I said my creaky, "Still twenty-five," he said, "Fabulous," a word I'd never heard him use, and he said it like he was imitating someone.

As usual, I carried my typewriter into the living room and returned to the kitchen.

He was reading the paper. Cynthia bent down and kissed his head. I saw him flinch.

. . . . .

Jack was talented at every art form. On the living-room wall, he'd painted a mural of the street outside—the trees and sidewalk, a boy on a skateboard, and a woman carrying a string bag full of groceries; it took me a week before I realized she was Cynthia. In his bedroom were dozens of framed black-and-white photographs he'd taken of his bed, rumpled and made.

Jack had gone to graduate school for architecture at Yale and to Harvard for art history, a year apiece; he'd written for a famous magazine and rocked in a band. Now he wanted to direct movies—or, as he called them, pictures.

He was working for a production company, but I kept realizing that I didn't know what he did, and every time he explained it to me,

I knew even less. All I'd remember were the names of famous actors he said were "attached" to movies his company would produce.

"Tell me what you do again," I said one night when he'd folded up the newspaper and Cynthia was putting a big bowl of pasta on the table. I said it because the kitchen felt quiet, and not in the nice way it had in the past; it was loud with quiet.

He said, "I'm a P.A.," and I could tell from his tone that was all he wanted to say.

I knew he was in a bad mood, but I was hoping to talk him out of it. I said, "Riddle me this, Batman: What does P.A. stand for?"

"Production assistant."

With all the surprise I felt, I said, "You're an assistant?"

He said, "Yup."

. . . . .

I always looked forward to the moment when Jack came home, and not just because it signaled the end of my typing day. Hearing him on the stairs, I'd think, *Let the fun begin!* But when he actually did walk in, the apartment itself seemed to tense up and go gloomy.

Now when Cynthia said, "Big Old Bear," she seemed to be trying to remind him of how he felt about her; she was asking him to be the *bar* of yesteryear.

I noticed that he didn't always answer her questions. He'd be reading the paper, and she'd say something ordinary, like, "What's the news of the day?" and silence would follow.

I knew she didn't care about the actual answer to her actual question; it was her way of saying, *Hello,* or even, *I love you.* When he didn't respond, she'd go back to washing her lettuce or sautéing onions, like she hadn't asked anything in the first place.

I told Josh about it, and his answer, a long blink followed by a blank expression, made me wonder if one day soon he'd stop answering my questions. So I said, "Don't you think that's rude?"

He sort of shrugged.

I was defending myself when I said, "It just seems wrong."

He said, "It's between them, though."

. . . . .

In a way, I hadn't really seen Jack up close before. He'd lived in the attic bedroom, which was like a separate house on top of ours. Then he went away to college, and he didn't always come home for vacations. He'd visit a girlfriend somewhere or go on a trip. Sometimes he'd promise to come home and then change his mind.

Once, when I'd been really disappointed, my father had tried to explain that I couldn't count on Jack the way I wanted to; I had to learn to appreciate him for what he could do and not be too crestfallen about what he couldn't.

I knew what my father meant. One year Jack drove a thousand miles to have dinner with our mother on her birthday; the next he didn't even call.

He loved doing huge favors and surprising people with his generosity. He liked going above and beyond the call of duty, but he didn't like duty itself.

It occurred to me that he might think I expected him to ask my typing score; anyway, he stopped asking.

This was a relief, since my score wasn't improving. How could I type all day, every day and not get better? The answer: I wasn't typing all day, every day. I'd started taking long breaks in the afternoon. I'd pack a sandwich and go to Washington Square Park, intending just to stay an hour. I'd linger awhile by the dog run, especially if there was a puppy. I'd sit by the dry fountain, where a comedian tried out jokes on the NYU students. I pretended to be one of them. Sometimes a mime performed. A voice in my head would nag me to get back to my typing, but another one would say, *Just a little longer.*

I might walk over to St. Marks Place and try on sunglasses that were displayed on tables. Or I'd get lost, looking at clothes in a boutique. I stayed out later and later until my goal was to get back to the apartment before Cynthia got home.

. . . . .

Josh and I went out to inexpensive restaurants—to La Rosita on Broadway for Cuban breakfasts, to V&T up by Columbia for pizza, to any place on East Sixth Street for Indian food, or to the Corner

Bistro on West Fourth for burgers. Every once in a while, though, he'd ask me to meet him at a nicer restaurant, and I came to realize that we went when he'd finished a poem. He'd read it to me during dessert, and I'd applaud and kiss him.

It was after one of those dinners that I finally worked up the courage to whimper in bed.

It felt like acting at first, but then it wasn't. It was great. At the end, I let out a big yell, which made me laugh afterward and say as a joke, "I came."

Josh was quiet. "Honey," he said, "I have roommates."

· · · · ·

One night before dinner, when Jack didn't answer Cynthia I glared at him, and he said, "What?"

I said, "Cynthia asked you a question."

He looked at me for a long moment, like he was trying to remember liking me. Then he turned around to Cynthia. With more affection than I'd heard in weeks, he said, "What was that, sugar pie?"

· · · · ·

She didn't come over the next night.

When Jack walked in and said, "What's the score?" I knew he was trying to make me feel that everything was all right, so I knew it wasn't.

"I didn't take a test today," I said. For the first time he was the one who carried my typewriter to the living room and stowed it under the coffee table.

"Chinese?" he said, and handed me a menu.

We agreed on a few dishes. He called and ordered. Then he sat down with his newspaper in the kitchen.

I went to the living room and opened the book on Edward Hopper.

He called out: "You're not going to keep my company?"

"I'll be there in a second," I said, but I didn't join him until our dinner was delivered. We unpacked the cartons and sat down at the table.

"Sophie," he said, once we were eating.

I kept my eyes on his hands as though absorbed in learning how to hold my chopsticks by watching him hold his. I said, "Uh-huh?"

He spoke slowly. "What happens between Cynthia and me is between Cynthia and me."

I knew he was right, and I felt embarrassed—and embarrassed to be embarrassed in front of him.

After a moment, I said, "Maybe I should stay somewhere else for a while."

He didn't answer right away. Then he said, "Where could you stay?"

I had a terrible feeling—*I don't have anywhere to stay.*

I'd gone to Robert's for dinner a couple of times, but I'd noticed that he only invited me when Naomi wasn't going to be there. I thought of my friends from college and pictured their apartments. No one had enough room for me or my clothes, and especially not for my huge typewriter.

I thought of Josh. Usually just the idea of him cheered me up. Right then, though, I experienced the sensation of being in love for the uncertainty that being in love is.

The only other possible host was Grandma Mamie. I still hadn't visited her. It was hard even to make myself call her every few weeks.

I said, "I could stay at Grandma Mamie's," hoping against hope that Jack would say, *Don't be ridiculous.*

· · · · ·

"Don't be ridiculous," he said during our farewell dinner, when I said the dress Cynthia gave me was too big a present for me to accept. It was a sample from her showroom, a dress made of blue-black wool jersey, which she said I could wear on job interviews.

I went to the bathroom to try it on. In the mirror, I saw that the dress was a little longer on one side. I didn't want to embarrass Cynthia, so I hunched my right shoulder and lowered my left to make the dress hang evenly.

Cynthia understood; she said, "It's cut on the bias," which meant that its unevenness was deliberate.

"It's great," Jack said.

. . . . .

Jack surprised me by offering to drive me up to my grandmother's. This was just the kind of favor Jack liked doing most. He was going to make a difficult thing fun. It was cold, but he put the top down on his convertible and turned the heat on. We drove along the river. The sky was a cold blue.

Grandma Mamie lived in the Riverdale section of the Bronx, one exit past the first toll on the Henry Hudson Parkway. When we got to her apartment house, Jack tipped the doorman so we could park in the circular drive, between NO PARKING ANYTIME signs.

Jack carried my big typewriter in the elevator. He hid while I rang my grandmother's doorbell.

When she opened the door, he showed her his handsome face.

She was thrilled to see it.

He was flirty with her, calling her Mamie instead of Grandma and telling her how fantastic she looked. He sat down and ate a pastry she'd made, a yellow briquette he proclaimed "delicious."

When it was time for him to go, I walked out with him. We stood by his car. I wanted to make a joke so that everything would be okay between us. I considered saying, "Thank you for opening your home to me," but it seemed like a joke at Robert's expense, and maybe bitter.

Instead, Jack spoke. He took both my hands in his and said, "I'm for you, and you're for me." This was something my uncle had said to me when I was little, and I hadn't heard it since and understood it only now.

Jack hugged me good-bye. He had a way of hugging that could pull you all the way in, and make you feel safer and more loved than you ever thought possible.

Then he got in his little car and was gone.

3.

MY GRANDMOTHER'S APARTMENT looked out on the Harlem River, which is no Hudson; our cut of the Harlem wasn't mighty or mythic, not blue or green or gray, but varying shades of brown that evoked no metaphor save human waste.

The apartment had two rooms and could feel spacious if you were the only one in it, which I never was except when my grandmother went downstairs for the mail or out to Gristedes for groceries.

She was on a perpetual diet and didn't eat dinner with me. Mostly she stood nearby, at the ready to refill my water glass or serve the seconds I never asked for.

I couldn't. Everything she made had been sautéed or boiled or baked too long. I could eat the salad—iceberg lettuce, mealy tomatoes, and carrot pennies smothered in lo-cal dressing—but the chicken was a dried-up dishrag and the baked potato a shiny sack of mush.

She kept calling me "Sophilla," her pet name for me, and the sound of it made me feel like a sack of mush myself.

She asked how Robert was, but it was Naomi she wanted to talk about. "She's a nice girl, Naomi," my grandmother said, her tone implying there was something more important that Naomi wasn't. "You can't blame her for wanting to get married."

I said, "I don't think Naomi's so interested in getting married," though I didn't know.

My grandmother turned her head to the side.

"Really," I said. "She's pretty busy with school."

She sat down with me and sighed. She sighed again and then said, "It's hard after college, Sophilla?"

I thought she was talking about finding a job, starting a new life, joining what we recent college graduates called "The Real World," and I agreed: It was hard.

"Not that it isn't hard in college," she said. "The boys want the younger girls."

I said, "Um."

"It gets harder, Sophie," she said, squinting at me, as though seeing despair and loneliness in my future. "Harder and harder."

"You know what?" I said. "I should practice my typing."

She told me that I'd practiced all day, and I had. But I cleared the dishes and wiped off the green place mat we'd agreed I'd use underneath the typewriter to protect the finish of her dining-room table. She wouldn't let me do the dishes.

Once I was sitting in front of the typewriter, she said, "I'm just trying to tell you how life is, Sophilla."

I didn't know what to say, so I said, "Thank you."

She said, "Maybe Jack or Robby could introduce you to someone."

I made my face say, *Hm,* and began to type.

. . . . .

I planned to call Josh once my grandmother went to bed, but she stayed where she was on the sofa, knitting an unwearable sweater of Orlon.

Josh was a maniac about sleep and I had to call him before eleven. At 10:55, I went into the bedroom and dialed. I only had time to say, "Hi," before she came in.

"Excuse me," she said and went to her closet.

Josh said, "How's it going?"

I said, "I'm here at my grandmother's," in a voice meant to convey both the hardship of this and her presence in the room.

He said, "How is she?"

. . . . .

Without comedians, mimes, or puppies to distract me, I broke through to thirty-two words the next day. I made a few calls and set up appointments. At dinner I was exultant. I ate the strings of what must once have aspired to be pot roast, and I was considering a second helping when my grandmother said, "You have to let people know you're looking, Sophilla."

Thinking she meant for a job, I was about to say, *I have,* but then I realized she was talking about men again. I said no to seconds and cleared the table, though she fought me on this and blocked the sink so I couldn't wash the dishes.

I was about to start an exercise on numbers, my nemesis, when she said, "Jack doesn't have any friends you could meet?"

Even as I said the words, "I did meet somebody," I regretted them and began typing up a storm of nonsense.

"Oh!" she said, pulling up a chair. "What's his name?"

"Josh," I said.

"Josh what, if you don't mind me asking?"

"Rudman."

"Jewish?" she said.

I said, "He is Jewish," though her pleasure in it rankled me. "I have to type."

"Excuse me," she said. "I didn't mean to bother you."

She returned an exercise later. "What does Josh do, if you don't mind me asking?"

"He's a poet," I said.

She didn't say anything.

"He writes poetry." I said, "He's really good," though I hadn't understood any of the poems he'd read to me.

She said, "This is his living?"

I told her that he programmed computers for a research group at Columbia Presbyterian.

"The hospital?" she said.

"Uh-huh."

She thought for a second. "Maybe he'll decide to go to medical school."

"He already went and didn't like it."

He'd said, "I realized I was too creative to be a doctor," which had bothered me; Robert was going to be a doctor. Remembering how I'd felt, I frowned.

To make me feel better my grandmother said, "He could change his mind."

"I don't think so."

She said, "You could talk to him."

I said, "I'm having dinner with him tomorrow," even though we hadn't made plans.

A little later, I went into the bedroom to call him. I told him that I would be in Manhattan for interviews the next day.

My grandmother walked into the bedroom and, seeing that I was on the phone, said, "Excuse me," and left.

She closed the door, but not all the way, and it occurred to me that she was standing on the other side.

I lowered my voice. "Maybe we could have dinner."

"I can't tomorrow," he said, and he named the ex-girlfriend he'd made plans with. One of his principles was that he maintained contact, as he called it, with his ex-girlfriends; another was that he did not cancel plans.

The phone sat on a stack of paperbacks, the entirety of my grandmother's library, and I chose this moment to read the titles. My eyes were on *Love's Urgent Flame* when Josh said, "What about Thursday?"—three nights away.

I had to force myself to return to the typewriter, and was almost grateful for my grandmother's interruption— "You know, Sophilla . . ."

I looked up.

"Grandpa wasn't interested in me at first," she said. "He had a lot of girls."

I'd heard this story maybe 250,000 times before. As she spoke, I mentally mouthed the details: My grandfather, whom for the purpose of the story she called Abie, was friendly with her brother and would come over to play cards Friday nights.

"When Abie walked in, I walked out," she said. "He thought I had a date. I was a very popular girl. I took myself to the movies," she said.

I said, "I think I understand what you're trying to say." I flipped to a new exercise.

"You've got to be a little smart, Sophie," she said.

"Got it," I said.

She was quiet after that, and when I glanced over at her, she looked worried.

At the end of the evening, I took a timed test. I'd typed thirty-six. I got into bed, thinking, *You typed thirty-six words per minute.* I closed my eyes, thinking, *Thirty-six, thirty-six, thirty-six.*

I was almost asleep when my grandmother said, "Sophie?"

"Yes?"

She said, "Maybe you should let Josh call *you* once in a while."

. . . . .

I couldn't wear my interview suit, as seersucker said "summer" as clearly as did corn on the cob and flip-flops; I was grateful for the dress Cynthia had given me, though in the mirror it looked more uneven than cut on the bias. I put on my trench coat. Remembering the blisters from my first interview, I placed my pumps in the cardboard accordion file with my envelope of résumés and wore sneakers.

My grandmother said, "You look like a little doll," which was not exactly the look I was striving for. Still, it was one of her highest compliments, along with, *You're a modern girl in every way.*

I tried to tell her that I wasn't having dinner with Josh until Thursday, but it seemed like proof that I should be faking dates and letting him call me.

All I could manage was, "I won't be too late."

. . . . .

I stood outside waiting for the express bus to Manhattan, and even in the morning sun I was cold. I had three interviews—on Fifty-third and Lexington, Sixteenth and Union Square West, and Sixth Avenue and Forty-eighth. Before and after each appointment, I changed my shoes on the sidewalk. I'd face the building and try not to notice people noticing me.

I thought the last interview of the day, with a Rogers alum, might be easier than the rest because he'd at least have heard of our alma mater, but Clay White seemed bored and annoyed from the start. All through the interview, he was occupied with a paper clip he was unbending into uselessness. After a half hour, holding the straightened paper clip he'd achieved between his thumb and index finger, he said, "Tell me again what you've been doing since graduation."

I said that I'd been learning how to type, and I tried to make this sound hilarious. I'd just begun to tell him about the patron saint of lost job-seekers when his phone rang.

I thought this interruption might be one of those serendipitous opportunities to discontinue a failing anecdote, but after he hung up he said, "You were saying?"

I told him that I'd heard her, "Can you type?" as, *Are you willing?* and delivered what I hoped would be an acceptable end of the story, if not the punch line: "Then she gave me the test."

"How'd you do?"

The effect of his question was to turn my anecdote back into a real experience: Once again, I saw the pencil counting up the words I'd typed and subtracting the errors I'd made; I knew that I hadn't done well but I was hoping, which struck me now as the basic emotion of my entire life.

I told Clay that I'd typed nine words a minute.

He said, "Call me when you get to forty."

I almost said that I was up to thirty-six now, but I liked not saying it better. Not saying it made me feel I would do fine without the help of Clay White.

Then I was outside on the sidewalk, changing from my pumps into sneakers.

· · · · ·

I turned off Sixth Avenue onto Forty-seventh Street and found myself in the diamond district as it was closing: Necklaces were removed from velvet necks and rings from velvet fingers; metal curtains and iron gates were pulled shut and locked. The people rushing by me looked cold and seemed more desperate to get away from where they were than eager to get to wherever they were going. I was cold myself, and my feet hurt from their brief imprisonment in pumps. My accordion file was weighed down with the publishers' catalogs I'd amassed. I'd been given at least one at the close of each interview, like a consolation prize—*I can't give you a job, but here is a catalog. Oh, thank you for this catalog.*

I'd already flipped through the catalogs, but I didn't know what to look for. What was I supposed to do with them? Throwing them out seemed like giving up.

Walking down Fifth Avenue, I couldn't work up any excitement about being in New York. It was hard to feel that anything was possible in a dress and sneakers. In a dress and sneakers, I was just me, pretending to be on a date while my boyfriend was having dinner with an ex-girlfriend. In a dress and sneakers, I was just me, killing time before going back to my grandmother's.

It began to rain, and I ducked into a phone booth. I told myself I was not going to call home, but I pictured it: My father would have pulled up the driveway a few minutes earlier, and now I knew he was standing in the kitchen having two fingers of gin with ice and hors d'oeuvres my mother had prepared for him, and they would be talking about the day. The kitchen would be warm, and there would be the smell of a well-cooked dinner almost finished.

My mother was the one who answered, and she accepted the charges. She must have heard the despair in my, "Hi"; she said, "I'll put your father on."

"Mom?" I asked her to send me a coat, and she said, "Of course."

I told my father everything, and I felt better just having him on the other end. He was quiet. My father listened more closely than anyone, so he didn't have to make the sounds of listening; he didn't say, "Uh-huh," or make comments, or ask questions.

When I finished, he told me what I already knew: Soon I would find a job and get an apartment of my own.

In the background, I heard my mother ask him to tell me that another overdue notice had come for *20th-Century Typewriting*, but he said, "Why don't you come home this weekend?" He made his voice light, like it might just be a good idea.

I thought how nice it would be to go home, but then it occurred to me how hard it might be to leave again.

"Think about it," he said. "We're here."

. . . . .

I typed furiously. I typed as though my life depended on it. I typed like a madwoman. Even with all of my errors to subtract, that afternoon I counted up forty-five words per minute.

I called the saint with my typing news, and she congratulated me and promised to keep me in mind. I called everyone I'd put off calling; I set up appointments with anyone who would see me.

Before dinner, I was lifting the typewriter off the table when my grandmother said that maybe I would have some news for her soon. I assumed that she meant about a job, and I said, "I hope so."

It was her smile that made me ask what she'd meant. "Maybe you'll get engaged," she said.

"Grandma," I said, and I turned full around to look at her. "I'm not ready to get married yet."

She said, "Why, if I may ask?"

"I'm just, you know, twenty-two."

She turned her head to the side.

I didn't know what to say. "I'm just starting my career."

She said, "Let me ask you a question."

"Okay."

"You like this Josh."

"Yes," I said.

"So?"

"So . . . ?" I said.

"You don't want to marry him?"

"Not now."

She nodded. "Let me ask you a question," she said again. "If a twenty-two-year-old girl met a nice Jewish guy who made a good living, she would be crazy not to marry him."

"I'm sorry," I said. "What was the question?"

"Does he want to marry you?"

"I don't know," I said, and I tried to make my tone say, *I don't care,* but just then I did.

. . . . .

I had three personnel interviews and aced each typing test, which filled me with pride.

In the late afternoon, I had an appointment with one of the editors from Jack's list. She said, "How's Jack?" like she didn't care, so I knew she did.

Her name was Honey Zipkin, and I thought of my grandmother saying, *You look like a little doll,* because Honey really did look like one. She was very pretty, but she had a bigger head than you'd expect on her little frame, plus long blond hair.

It wasn't until close to the end of the interview that she told me she needed an assistant. She gave me a manuscript, pages in a box, to critique over the weekend.

I had an hour before I had to meet Josh, and I walked up Park Avenue. Catching sight of Grand Central, and the big clock and the statue on the roof, I got this huge feeling: *This is your life, Sophie Applebaum.*

Soon I would be working as an editorial assistant in a major publishing house. I would be leaving the dull brown Bronx for sparkling, silvery Manhattan. I would be moving into my own apartment.

And, I thought, *I am about to have dinner with the man I love.*

Outside Szech West, I changed from sneakers into pumps.

Josh sat at a corner table, studying a page of the yellow legal pad he wrote poems on. He stood up and gave me a kiss that was more suited to a cheek than lips; his embrace seemed to be holding me off instead of pulling me in.

I reminded myself that this was Josh: He was reserved; I couldn't take his personality personally.

He picked up his menu and, handing me mine, said, "I need food." He seemed to think of being hungry or tired as an early stage of illness.

After we'd ordered, he reached for my hand and held it. "How's your grandmother?"

"Hard," I said.

He nodded, which was how he told me to go on.

"I don't know." I said, "She's always talking to me about getting married," and I looked at his face to see if there was anything on it for me to know.

"You should ask her about her life," he said. "Where she came from. That's what I talk to Bubbe about."

Up until that moment, I'd been at the earliest stage of love, when you feel it will turn you into the person you want to be. Now, his gentle voice and sage advice took me to a later stage: I felt I needed to pretend to be a better person than I was so he'd keep loving me. This was hard because it made me hate him.

I couldn't look into his eyes, so I looked down at his hand. I'd never said anything about the turquoise ring he wore; usually, I tried not to notice it. "Where'd you get the ring?" I asked.

He said, "I bought it myself in Santa Fe."

I nodded. It was good that the ring had not been given to him by one of the ex-girlfriends he maintained contact with. But, like Josh, I had principles, and one of mine was that, except for a watch and a plain gold wedding band, a man ought not to wear jewelry. A ring, even this small and un-diamond, put him in a country that a man in a fur coat ruled.

"You don't like it?" he said.

"No," I said. "I like turquoise."

. . . . .

I spent all day reading the manuscript I would have to report on. It was a novel called *The Wives of Armonk*, about women with a lot of money and how they liked to spend it plus have affairs with young men who had big penises. The main character, Jacqueline, fell in love with the pool man. He was skimming the pool for leaves, and she dived in naked. Then they were in the pool house, and she was saying, "Yes . . . yes . . . oh, Lord . . . yes."

At dinner, my grandmother said, "So," and I could tell she was about to bring up Josh.

"You know what I was just thinking?" I said. "I don't know too much about your childhood."

"I was a little girl," she said, and I realized I'd asked her this question before. She sometimes said she grew up in Austria, other times Germany, and once Poland, and she'd left when she was twelve, fourteen, and sixteen. Her family was always very poor, but sometimes her father was a shoemaker and other times a farmer.

"What was your father like?" I asked.

"Sick," she said.

"What was wrong with him?"

Tapping her chest, she said, "Weak lungs."

Finally I asked why she didn't like talking to me about her past. "Is it painful?"

"To tell you the truth," she said, "I don't remember."

. . . . .

I was a slow reader, and I didn't start writing my report until midnight on Sunday. I stayed up all night and at sunrise saw the Harlem River turn unscenically from black to brown.

I proofread my report twice and was especially proud of the last line: "This is dreck."

I didn't have time to take a shower, change my clothes, or put in my contact lenses. I took the express bus down to Manhattan and got to Steinhardt Publishers just before five.

The receptionist asked for my name, and I told her.

As she picked up the phone, I said, "I'm just supposed to drop this off."

She said, "I'll tell Honey you're here," and a moment later, out came Honey.

"Come on back," she said, taking the manuscript and my reader's report from me.

Incoherent with sleeplessness, I tried to apologize for wearing jeans.

She shook her head like I was a little crazy.

I sat in her office while she read my report. She tipped herself back in her chair and her eyes widened as she read. Then she laughed.

I hadn't made any jokes in my report.

She laughed and laughed, and when she could speak, she told me Steinhardt was publishing *The Wives of Armonk*.

"Oh," I said. "Sorry."

She said, "No." Then she asked me when I could start.

· · · · ·

When I gave my grandmother the news, she said, "How much are they paying you, if you don't mind me asking?"

The salary was very low, and I didn't want to say the number out loud. Instead, I told her what my father had told me: I was an apprentice, learning a craft.

She turned her head to one side.

I was too tired and too happy to let this bother me. I said, "Maybe I'll cook you dinner one night before I go."

She said, "That's nice," but I could see she didn't care for the idea.

She sat down with me on the sofa, where I was splayed out in my exhausted bliss.

She said, "I bet you'll be happy to leave your old grandma."

"No," I said. "No." *Yes, yes,* I thought in the cadence of an Armonk wife, *oh, Lord . . . yes.*

When she began to ask me about Josh, I said, "Listen, Mamie." I looked at her, old lady to old lady, and said, "I don't want to talk about my romantic life." It occurred to me that *romantic life* was the phrase you'd use if you didn't have one; for a moment, I went back to the night when I'd faked a date with Josh and wandered around midtown in the rain.

"Why," she said, "if you don't mind me asking?"

"I don't know," I said. "It makes me feel bad."

She took one of my cigarettes and lit it. She puffed but didn't inhale. It reminded me of a picture she had of herself with my grandfather in a nightclub. They were sitting at a big round table, and she was wearing a shiny dress and lipstick.

"I'm trying to tell you how life is," she said.

I said, "Things have changed, though." I tried to make my voice sound certain. "Things are different."

"How?" she said.

I thought of the professor who taught Introduction to Women's Studies at Rogers and tried to think of some sure, smart thing she would say. Instead, I remembered that she'd broken her foot and even once the cast came off she walked with a cane. For some reason, this seemed to weaken my case. "Women have careers now," I said. "We don't care as much about, you know, men."

"Is that so?"

I wanted to give her a specific example of my new modern relationship with Josh, but all I could think of was that we split the check. It was his idea, an offshoot of the principle that everything should be equal between us. When the check came, Josh divided it, calculating how much more my soda and coffee were. He himself drank only water.

"Anyway," I said, "I don't want to talk about it."

She got up from the sofa and went to the kitchen. In a few minutes my dinner was set out.

I said, "Thank you."

"You're welcome."

For the first time, she didn't sit down with me or hover nearby. She turned on the television and pretended to watch it.

The chicken was undercooked; it was pink inside. I considered putting it back in the oven, but I didn't. I got up from the table and hid the chicken underneath other garbage in the pail. I cleared my dishes and washed them, without any protest from her.

"I'm going to take a walk," I said.

She said, "Have a good time."

I went across the street to the pizza place and ordered a slice. I sat there eating it under fluorescent lights. The only other diners were an old man and a young couple with a child who whined. They didn't seem unhappy or happy. It was impossible to learn anything from looking at them.

Sitting there, I thought of my grandmother saying, *I only want what's best for you,* and I knew that if I could get myself to believe this

I'd feel better about her and myself. But like everything else I was supposed to think, it didn't feel true.

· · · · ·

Robert called to congratulate me on my job and asked if I'd have dinner with him and Naomi. Jack was coming, too. "Bring Josh if you
want to," Robert said.

When I mentioned the invitation to Josh, he said that he was at a
critical stage with a poem, but if the dinner was important to me
he'd go.

He seemed to be stating a principle of his, though I wasn't sure exactly what it was and didn't ask. Lately, his principles had begun to
feel like bars on a cage I was supposed to fit inside.

I said, "It's not important."

· · · · ·

At Robert's, Naomi gave me a hug, and I thought, *Is all forgiven?* In
the kitchen, I saw that Robert's MEAT and MILK labels were still on the
drawers and cabinets.

There were only four places set at the table, so I knew Cynthia
wasn't coming, and Jack himself came late. He walked in tired and full
of jokes about what he called "the shoot."

I asked him what the movie was about, and he said that the shoot
was for a commercial.

"I thought you made movies," I said.

He said that commercials were the company's bread and butter.

Robert and Naomi had cooked a big dinner, a lamb stew and some
mushy starch that was supposedly Middle Eastern and made me think
the two of them and my grandmother could benefit from a cooking
lesson from Cynthia.

Robert kept smiling at me in what felt like the private way of our
pre-Naomi past. I thought maybe he was proud of me for finally getting a job.

I mentioned that my new boss was an old girlfriend of Jack's.

Jack said, "How did you know that?"

I said, "She wouldn't stop talking about you."

Robert sounded like a little boy when he said, "Were you nice to her?"

Jack said, "I satisfied her needs"—I think to mortify Naomi.

But Naomi stood up to him; she said, "How do you mean, Jack?"

At dessert, Robert came out with a bottle of champagne.

I thought it was sweet of him to celebrate my job, and I was about to say so when he held up his glass and announced his engagement to Naomi.

I made my mouth smile, say, "Wow," and kiss them both.

It was hard not to feel happy for Robert, though, since he seemed so happy for himself. It reminded me of the way he'd looked in the mirror when I'd helped him get ready for his prom.

Seeing himself in his tuxedo, he'd said, "Good, right?"

. . . . .

Jack and I walked out together and down Broadway.

I had keys to Josh's apartment; I was supposed to meet him there after dinner. I knew he was probably already home from the library, but when Jack asked if I needed to rush off to Ovid I said that I didn't.

We went to a bar on Broadway, and Jack ordered scotch for both of us. I pulled out a cigarette, and Jack took my matches and struck one for me. We sat there with our drinks and didn't talk at first, which felt nice.

"Well," he said, "there goes our little boy."

I remembered Jack saying, *What happens between me and Cynthia is between me and Cynthia,* so I hesitated before saying, "What's wrong with Cynthia?"

He said, "There's not a thing wrong with that woman."

"I mean, why didn't she come?"

He thought for a moment. Then he told me that he'd suspected Robert's announcement. "I think Cynthia wants to get married."

"Oh," I said. "Do you want to marry her?"

He said, "I am giving it some very serious thought," but the way he said it made me think he wasn't.

I remembered my father's speech about what Jack was capable of

and wasn't; he'd said, *It has nothing to do with how much Jack loves you.*
I thought about all the girls he'd stopped loving; it was like he had a
timer, and at a certain point it just buzzed.

I said, "Does she say she wants to get married?"

"She's from Alabama," he said. "She doesn't talk like that."

"So, how do you know?"

"She's thirty-two," he said.

"That sounds like something Grandma would say."

"Which one?" he said.

I knew he was just dodging the topic, but I answered anyway.
"Mamie. Obviously."

We'd finished our scotches and he raised his hand to the bartender;
I thought he was going to signal for the check, but he pointed to our
glasses: *Another round.*

Then he laughed, and his mood got about a hundred pounds
lighter. "I can't believe you're going to work for Honey Zipkin."

I said, "What happened with you two?"

"Not what she wanted to happen."

"Meaning?"

He said, "I didn't fall in love with her."

· · · · ·

I let myself into Josh's apartment. I was a little drunk. I stood in the
hall waiting for the bathroom for a long time before I figured out that
the door was just closed and no one was inside.

When I got into bed beside Josh, I put my arms through his and
kissed the back of his neck.

"You smell like a bar," he said.

I thought, *You smell like a library.* But I wanted to have sex right
then, so I said, "You smell like a poem."

· · · · ·

"I'm trying to think of Naomi as Robert's first wife," I said to Josh.
We were having breakfast at La Rosita.

He looked at me with something like disapproval, and I was surprised to feel disapproval right back at him.

"That was a joke," I said.

"But you don't like her."

"I don't like her yet," I said. "But maybe I will."

"I think you should at least pretend to like her," he said. "She's going to be a member of your family."

I was getting that caged feeling again. But right then I saw my key. When the check came, I said, "This is on me."

· · · · ·

Jack told me about the apartment, a walk-up above a cigar store on Thirty-third Street. Maura Edwards had made documentaries all over the world; now she was going to New Jersey to have a baby and needed to sublet her apartment.

When I met her at the apartment, she was eight months' pregnant, and her skin was waxy and pale. She said, "You're on time," but her intonation said, *You're late*.

She said the apartment was her refuge and spoke of it with more affection than she did either the boyfriend she was moving in with or the baby she was about to have. Her voice was almost loving when she said that the apartment had no bugs. A gecko she'd brought back from Brazil ate them. He lived in the walls.

Even by New York standards the apartment was tiny, and the few pieces of furniture were child-sized, which made the apartment feel like a dollhouse—or doll cell—though the intention was obviously to make the apartment seem bigger. What made the apartment seem smaller was that everywhere, on every surface, were vases and sculptures, tchotchkes galore.

She seemed deflated when I agreed to the terms of the sublet: It might last a month or a year, she said; she might want to use the apartment herself sometimes, and if she did she'd give me twenty-four hours' notice and a rent reduction.

Since it was an illegal sublet, I was to make myself as invisible as possible. If anyone asked, I was her sister. I couldn't receive mail here, and I would have to forward hers.

I said, "No problem," and explained that I could easily send it from my office, which was just a few blocks away.

She wasn't listening. She was resigned now, showing me how to work the answering machine, though a moment later she asked me never to touch it. She played the outgoing message she'd recorded, which was in English first and Spanish second and gave her phone number in New Jersey. She seemed to be concentrating as she listened to her own voice, as though it might have something important to tell her.

She was more sure of herself than anyone I'd ever met, except maybe my father. You could tell that she'd gotten camera crews on overbooked flights all over the world and knew when to stand up to a customs official and when to offer a bribe. Her voice was full of certainty, even when she said, after good-bye, "I have no idea what I'm doing."

· · · · ·

I put my typewriter way in the back of my grandmother's closet. It took up a lot of room, but she didn't have many shoes. I promised that I'd come back for it soon. "I'll borrow Jack's car," I said, even though he'd never lent it to me and I doubted that he would.

I was putting my bags by the door when my grandmother said, "You're a modern girl in every way."

I wasn't too sure about that, but I thanked her. "Well, roomie," I said.

She looked upset, and I thought that maybe she'd heard my "roomie" as *roomy,* as in big and fat, so I said, "Roomie as in roommate."

Her face didn't change.

I was happy, and maybe it made her see how unhappy I'd been living with her. Or, knowing that her life lectures hadn't stuck, maybe she was envisioning my impending spinsterhood.

She double-sighed, and in a voice that sounded as sad as she looked, she said, "The world is your oyster."

I'd heard the expression, of course, and I knew it was supposed to refer to pearls to come. But it made me think of an actual oyster, and picturing the hard gray shell and the slimy animal inside, I thought, *My world* was *like an oyster, but not anymore.*

4.

AT 375 MADISON AVENUE, Steinhardt Publishers occupied three floors of a building that had once been grand. Like a faded beauty trying to conceal her age, the lobby was lit dimly; your eyes acknowledged the gold-domed ceiling and marble walls without really seeing them. The red exit sign glowed like a night-light.

I worked on the floor the elevators called 14, though it came right after 12. My desk was one of five in a makeshift secretarial pool we called the Cave, short for Bat Cave. Floor-to-ceiling file cabinets blocked all sunlight; the shredding carpet was variegated with the splash patterns of spilled coffee.

I shared the Cave with three girls and one Boy Wonder, Adam, whom I adored. He was the kind of man who might've fished Zelda Fitzgerald out of the fountain at the Plaza, draped his cashmere coat around her shoulders, never asked for it back, and never told anyone the story. He was slight, with a hairline well into recession even at twenty-two, but his character was so impeccable, his manner so graceful, that even then, when I saw him every day, I thought of him as tall and strikingly handsome.

With endless patience, he answered all my questions, even those I was too embarrassed to ask. This was lucky, as I was scared of Bettina, who'd already acquired a novel; once a week or so she'd shush us and announce, "I'm calling my author." Sue, a broad-backed workhorse from Minnesota, was perpetually on the phone with her boyfriend, a sophomore at what she called "the U." When they argued, as they often did, she didn't talk at all; she was a silent fumer. The phone wedged between her ear and shoulder, she typed letters and logged manuscripts, waiting for her boyfriend to grow up.

I sat across from Francine Lawlor—our desks touched—but whole days went by without our eyes even meeting. She was pale and thin, with pale, thin hair and pale, thin lips she pursed. A dozen years earlier, she'd arrived at Steinhardt to learn that the editor she'd been hired to assist had been fired. During what should have been a brief bossless interim, a position had been created for her. Now she was thirty-three, and Floating Assistant was still her title.

· · · · ·

My apartment was only seven minutes from Steinhardt, which gave me a fighting chance of being on time, though I usually wasn't. If Honey noticed, she didn't complain. She herself got to work practically at dawn, but her office, at the end of the Hall of Grown-ups, was the farthest from the Cave. If she wanted me, she called rather than walked down.

I opened her mail; I answered her phone; I typed her letters. Instead of asking me to read manuscripts, she said, "Take a look." Sent by lesser agents and friends of friends, these were the manuscripts she herself didn't want to read; early on, I understood that my job was to tell her that she didn't have to. A few weeks after she gave a manuscript to me, I'd return it to her with a typed rejection letter for her to sign. I used the language she herself used: "This story isn't quite compelling enough"; "The characters don't quite come alive"; or the ever-popular "This isn't quite right for our list," whatever that meant.

· · · · ·

Those first weeks I worried about how to dress for work. I looked to my fellow Cave-dwellers for guidance.

Invariably, Adam wore a starched button-down Oxford-cloth shirt, khakis, and a black—not blue—blazer, his urbane twist on the classic ensemble.

Bettina had mastered the look of a bad girl from a good girls' school—a cashmere twinset with a miniskirt or a crisp little blouse slyly unbuttoned just enough to whisper, *Lacy bra*.

Sue favored fuzzy angora sweaters in Easter's palette.

Francine Lawlor alternated between two suits—one gray, the other a startling red-orange and with them, she wore fluffy once-white blouses, the worst of which had a Louis XIV flap she decorated with a Phi Beta Kappa pin. She wore coffee-colored panty hose and navy blue pumps, low of heel, round of toe.

· · · · ·

As floating assistant, Francine was supposed to help us when we were busy, but we never asked and she never offered.

Mostly, she devoted herself to slush, the unending supply of unsolicited manuscripts sent by authors. No one cared about slush except as carton upon carton of it narrowed the hall where the copier lived; no one appreciated Francine's work except as it widened the path.

· · · · ·

One rainy lunch, Bettina decided we should take turns reading slush aloud. She opened a fresh carton and handed out a manuscript apiece to Adam, Sue, herself, and me.

It seemed rude to leave Francine out, so I asked if she wanted to read one.

She barely shook her head, so anathema was the idea to her.

Bettina laughed as she flipped through her manuscript and said, "I'll start." She read a sex scene from a wild Western, making her voice twangy for the cowboy, who hollers, "Ride me, baby bitch."

Adam read: " 'The witty journalists walked down Madison Avenue, where cabs swarmed like fireflies.' " He stood and raised his hand in imitation of hailing a taxi and called, "Firefly!"

Sue was about to read when her phone rang.

I got a dull thriller; every other paragraph began, "And then suddenly." Before reading, I happened to look over at Francine. Her face was stricken.

"Is this mean?" I said.

Bettina said, "Oh, shut up."

On principle, I returned the manuscript to the carton; the principle was I couldn't stand being told to shut up.

Adam backed me up, though: "She's right."

· · · · ·

Bettina said that Francine lived in the Cave and went through our desks at night.

Adam said, "What makes you say that?"

"She's always the first in," Bettina said, "and always the last to leave."

"That's your proof?" he said.

Bettina didn't answer.

"Take it back," he said, and he kept saying it until she did.

But Francine did seem guilty of something, even if it was just hating the rest of us.

5.

AFTER ABOUT A MONTH, Honey came alive to my many failings, namely that I was slow—slow at reading, slow at typing, slow at understanding her directions—and her noticing how slow I was only made me slower.

A letter that would have previously taken me a morning to type now took an entire day, and looking over that letter, Honey remarked not only on how long it had taken me to do but how badly it was done; suddenly, she was anti-Wite-Out.

When she gave me a stack of manuscripts, she now told me when they were to be read by, and each "Monday" or "Wednesday" or "Friday" seemed to be a reprimand for how long I'd taken in the past.

One afternoon when I returned a manuscript to Honey, she read my rejection letter and looked up at me. "Why?" she said.

"Why . . . ?"

"Why isn't *Temple of Gossamer* right for our list?"

By then Adam had explained that "our list" meant the books Steinhardt published, though I had no idea what unified them, except that they were books I wouldn't want to read. By that criterion, *Temple of Gossamer* fit our list perfectly.

Usually impatient, Honey now seemed to have all of eternity to wait for my answer.

I said the only thing I could think of: "It's bad."

Honey turned the cover of the manuscript over and took a look for herself. I stood there while she read, not sure whether I was supposed to stay or go. Finally, she stopped reading and said, "Okay."

She told me that if I was having trouble keeping up with my reading or typing I could always ask Clarisse for help—Clarisse was what Honey called Francine.

I nodded, as though I was on my way to ask Clarisse for help right now.

. . . . .

One morning I opened Honey's mail to find a letter from a Jenny Ling, who said how nice it had been to talk to Honey; she'd enclosed her résumé, "as promised."

I felt like I'd caught my boyfriend flirting with another girl and re-flexively threw the letter and résumé in the garbage.

Right away I was horrified at myself and fished them out.

I went down the hall, past the restrooms, supply closet, and mystery doors, and opened the one that led to the tiny balcony where Adam and I smoked cigarettes.

I smoothed out Jenny Ling's résumé. An editorial assistant only since June, Jenny had managed to acquire one novel and line edit two others she mentioned by name. She'd been the editor of a literary magazine at Yale, from which she'd graduated magna cum laude. Here, the résumé got a little repetitive—honors, honors, honors.

Her résumé put Lisa Michele Butler's to shame, but it was Jenny's cover letter that got to me: The girl claimed she could type sixty-five words per minute. I stared at that sixty-five until I finished smoking my cigarette, and went back to the Cave.

Adam must've seen how sick I felt; he looked at me for a long moment before turning to the crumpled papers I'd handed him.

He skimmed the résumé and letter and said, "I think Miss Ling will be fine without our help."

"I am going to Hell," I said.

"You're Jewish," he said. "You can't go to Hell."

I said, "You can if you're really assimilated."

I didn't throw the letter and résumé away; I couldn't. I filed them in my TO FILE file, where I put everything that I would figure out later; it was huge.

All that day I was so intent on avoiding Honey that I didn't realize she'd been avoiding me until she called. It was just after five. She said, "Can you come see me for a minute?"

I said, "Sure," which was what I always answered when I wanted to answer no.

After I hung up, I didn't move. It seemed possible that in a few minutes my life was going to change, and I wanted to stay on this side of it for as long as I could.

Adam was on the phone, going over copyediting changes with an author. In the tone of repeating what had just been said to him, he said: "Page one-forty-three, the penultimate paragraph, third line from the top, delete the comma."

As ever, Sue was on the phone, and I could tell by her posture—she was half lying on the desk—that she was crying. I knew this was not distress but joy: She always cried when her boyfriend admitted that he was a complete idiot.

It took me a second to register that Francine was looking at me. There might've been concern in her face, or maybe it was curiosity; she looked away too fast for me to tell.

Honey was on the phone, and I stood just outside her door, acknowledging myself as second fiddle to the fiddle she was talking to.

She said a Sweet 'n Low, "Have a good weekend," into the phone and a pesticidal, "Close the door, please," to me.

"Hi," I said.

She swiveled her chair sideways so she was facing the wall instead of me. I got her profile: *Honey in thought.*

"Sophie," she said, her eyes on the wall.

I waited. When she didn't say anything, I said, "Yes?"

"Sophie," she said again.

She swiveled face-front now and looked at me.

I nodded, *I'm ready.*

"I don't expect you to come in when I do," she said, and for the first time it occurred to me that she did. "But you come in later than anyone else," she said. "You're the last one in every day."

I did not nod.

She said, "Do you know what that says?"

I didn't; I didn't even know if it was a rhetorical question.

"You're telling Bettina and Sue and Adam and Clarisse that you're special."

I thought, *I'm not telling anyone anything unless I'm talking in my sleep.*

"You're telling Wolfe that you don't care about your job."

His full name was Bernard Wolfe, but no one called him Bernard or Bernie. Wolfe was quiet and humble and seemed less like an editorial director than a clerk in a used-record store. The prospect of him noticing me—even because I was late—was exciting, but I kept it off of my face, as I waited for Honey to tell me what my lateness told her.

She was rubbing her thumb and fingers together the way people usually do when they're miming money; she'd told me that handling books all day made her hands feel dirty, even if they looked clean. She was taking a good long look at me. "Why *are* you late every day?"

I panicked. I didn't really know why I was late. The only reason I could give was that I had trouble deciding what to wear. I tried to think of a reason that would make Honey say, *Well, why didn't you tell me before?* But what would that reason be? *I'm taking care of my aging parents? I have three small children? I'm blind?*

I said, "I'm sorry," and when it didn't seem to have any effect, I said it again.

Honey nodded, still waiting for an explanation. After another minute, though, she seemed to give up. She smiled at me then, and I had no idea why; it wasn't a genuine smile, or a happy one. I guessed that it meant, *Don't be afraid,* and I made myself smile back, *Okay.*

But my smile made hers disappear. "This is serious, Sophie."

I let my face become as grave as I felt. I said, "I will come in earlier."

· · · · ·

I'd believed my vow in Honey's office, but reporting back to my sympathizers in the Cave, I knew I couldn't change for Honey.

"You'll just come in earlier," Sue said. In her face I could see both the weariness of her daylong phone fight and relief at its resolution.

"What difference does it make what time you come in?" Bettina said, picking up the phone to make a call. "She is such a bitch."

Francine had stopped typing, and Adam and I noticed at the same moment. She immediately started up again, probably typing, *zzuuwwxxyy.*

Adam said one word to me and that was: "Cocktail."

. . . . .

He took me to a hotel bar with murals painted by Ludwig Bemelmans, the author and illustrator of the *Madeline* books I'd grown up with.

Adam ordered a martini for himself and one for me, the first of my life. While I sipped, he came up with lines in the cadence of the *Madeline* books:

> In the middle of the night,
> Honey Zipkin turns on the light,
> It's time for work, and sneakers on,
> she braves the day and Wolfe and dawn.

I felt better; then I remembered Honey saying, *Why* are *you late?*

Adam saw the change in my face and told me to try not to take Honey's behavior personally; he'd seen her pull this with another assistant. "She found fault with everything the poor girl did," he said. "Sheila."

"Was she fired?"

"Not exactly," Adam said. "She didn't come back from lunch."

"Then what?"

"Then nothing," he said. "Sheila was . . . troubled."

I said, "I am troubled."

He smiled and shook his head.

I wanted to be like Adam, and yet after a few sips of my second martini, I said a sloppy, "I suck at being an editorial assistant."

"You lack artifice," he said. "You lack the instinct to be a good slave."

This wasn't a bad way to think about it, but it didn't take me off Honey's hit list. I asked if he'd ever had trouble with his boss.

"Lord, no," he said. "But Wolfe is Wolfe and Honey is Honey."

Adam insisted on paying the check. Outside he said, "Shall I put you in a firefly?"

.   .   .   .   .

I met Josh at the Paris Theater. I was late, but no matter: The movies Josh wanted to see were the ones no one else did; we had the theater almost to ourselves.

I could tell by the quick kiss he gave me and the way he drew back that he was annoyed—either at my lateness or at the martini on my breath. He was quiet, which was his way of saying I'd done him wrong.

Afterward, we walked toward the subway, not holding hands.

It was January, and Josh and I were pale and cold, and it seemed to me just then that our lives were smaller than they had to be. We were a check split down the middle.

He was unlocking the door to his apartment when he said, "I wish you'd be on time."

I thought, *Who doesn't?*

I knew I was supposed to say I was sorry, but I'd already used up my *I'm sorry* allowance for the day.

In bed, he switched off the light and turned to the wall, away from me. Once my eyes adjusted to the dark, I saw that he'd put his second pillow on top of his head, like a sandwich, to drown out the sounds of the city so he could sleep.

I lay there thinking that I did not deserve this punishment. I'd only been a few minutes late, and early enough to see all the previews of the movies I didn't want to see and, with the way things were going, never would.

Then I thought of him waiting outside the Paris. He'd probably looked at his watch about a hundred times. Maybe he'd worried about me. As he waited, he might've wondered if I cared about him.

When I looked over at him, he'd taken the pillow off his head and was lying open-faced.

I said, "I'm sorry," and hearing myself say these words made me feel better.

. . . . .

I worried all weekend about being late on Monday. I didn't stay over at Josh's Sunday night because I was afraid I wouldn't be able to sleep, which was what happened at my own apartment.

I was awake at two A.M. and then three and then four, thinking how much slower and dumber I'd be the next day.

I woke up at eleven.

I knew everyone was still in the editorial meeting, where I should've been, but I called Honey's line and then Adam's, and each time the call was bounced to Irene at reception; when she answered, "Steinhardt," I hung up.

I took a shower; I made coffee; I hyperventilated.

Just before noon, Adam answered: "Editorial."

"I overslept," I said.

"I am going to hang up now," he said, "and walk down the hall to tell Honey that your grandmother died."

. . . . .

I got to work early on Tuesday; only Francine beat me. So I knew that she was the one who'd turned on my tensor lamp, simulating my early arrival, as she would every day from then on. She was eating a butter sandwich that she'd brought from home, and when she looked up I thanked her with my face, and she nodded.

Honey came down to the Cave a little while later.

She half sat on the edge of my desk and said, "This was the grandmother you stayed with?"

I couldn't lie into her eyes, so I lowered my head, as though in grief. "Uh-huh."

It seemed possible that my lie would bring on my grandmother's death. For a moment I felt like she had died, and I wished I'd been nicer to her in her lifetime. I thought, *She only wanted what was best for you.*

Honey said, "I'm so sorry, Sophie."

I said, "Thank you."

When I looked up, Francine was trying to conceal a smile, the first I'd ever seen.

. . . . .

By Thursday, Honey and I were back to normal.

She handed me a paper-clipped wad of receipts so I could compile her expense report to send to our business office in New Jersey; she said, "I want this to go out in the noon pouch."

I said, "I will do it right away." Everything I said to her now sounded like a written pledge.

I did do it right away and as fast as I could. I put all the slips in chronological order, hailing taxi receipts for every lunch and dinner and drink date and copying them all onto the request-for-reimbursement form. Bettina was away from her desk, so I couldn't ask to borrow her calculator; I did my own math.

When I returned to Honey's office, she was on the phone but, seeing the form in my hand, motioned me in and signed it.

I took the form down to Wolfe's office for his signature.

His door was open, but all I could see were his long, long legs, stretched way, way out onto the coffee table. Wolf was about nine feet tall and one inch thick; basically, he was flat.

I knocked on the door, and he told me to come in. He had a manuscript on his lap.

I said, "Hey."

He said, "Hey, Sophie," with warmth I'd never heard from him before.

He reminded me of someone Jack might've been friends with in high school. I could picture teenaged Wolfe walking past my childhood bedroom and saying, *Hey, Sophie,* like I might be someone he'd want to talk to if he didn't have a gig playing air guitar to a Jimi Hendrix record upstairs with my brother.

I stood there while he looked over Honey's expenses.

He had music playing on his stereo, and I recognized *Kind of Blue,* which Jack had given me for my birthday.

I said, "That's my favorite jazz tape," though as soon as I said, *jazz tape,* I worried that I'd given myself away as someone who owned only one.

He said, "Want to listen to it at lunch?"

"Okay," I said, cool as a jazz aficionado.

He signed the form, handed it back to me, and said he'd order sandwiches in for us, and what kind did I want?

I said, "What're you having?"

He thought a minute, in imitation of making a large decision, and said he would order turkey on pumpernickel with tomato and onion and Russian dressing.

"Two," I said.

"Pickles?"

I said, "Obviously."

I went back to my desk and sat there, feeling better than I had in weeks. I'd been waiting for something good to happen to me, and here it was. After Wolfe called to tell me that our turkeys had arrived, I didn't hurry to his office; I took a minute to appreciate the full pleasure and anticipation of what I was about to do. Walking down the hall, I thought, *You are walking down the hall to Wolfe's office for lunch.*

He was taking our sandwiches out of the bag.

He said, "Come on in," at the same time he picked up the phone and dialed, which was what Honey did; *Come in and sit here while I talk on the phone.*

But Wolfe was calling Irene; he told her that he was going into a meeting and to hold his calls, please.

After he hung up, he said, "You have something to read?"

"Right," I said.

When I returned with a manuscript, Wolfe was sitting on the sofa, his sandwich set out on the coffee table; mine was on the desk. Was I supposed to sit on the sofa beside him or in one of the chairs opposite his desk? *Sofa or chair, sofa or chair?*

I sat down on the chair.

He put on the record, and went back to the sofa and put his feet up on the coffee table. "Put your feet up, if you want to." That was the last thing he said. When I turned around, he was reading.

I did the same. I stopped only to lift my head as though appreciating the nuances of the music.

When the first side of the record finished, he walked over to the stereo, saying, "You know, Miles recorded this in a single session."

I said, "You're kidding," though it hadn't occurred to me that any record took more than one session.

I was noticing the picture on his desk. It was a girl who looked like him, just as skinny, with his bulging eyes and kindling for arms, except she wore her hair in braids. She had only one boot on and was reaching for the other and laughing. There were mountains in the background, and she was sitting by a campfire.

Before he picked up his manuscript again, I said, "Who's the happy camper?"

He didn't answer right away, and I worried that I'd made a mistake. It was wrong to talk while the music was playing or wrong to ask personal questions.

"That's my sister." He hesitated. "Juliet."

I didn't know what to say, and I considered saying nothing, and later wished I had. "Where does she live?"

He seemed to think for a minute; I thought maybe he was trying to remember her address. Then he shook his head.

I was about to say, "I'm sorry"; the words were forming in my mouth at the exact moment that I heard them come out of his.

He said, "I'm sorry about your grandmother, Sophie."

· · · · ·

I took Friday off for the funeral.

I slept late, and spent the day reading two manuscripts I'd brought home with me. Honey had marked them "Wednesday," and I wondered if when I turned them in on Monday she'd think I was two days early or realize that I was five late.

All that afternoon I worried about work and Honey, and it spread over to Josh. I hadn't told him how much trouble I was in, which made me feel that I was lying to him, which made me feel that he loved me under false pretenses, which made me feel that he did not really love me.

It was because I felt so tenuously loved that I arrived at the restaurant almost a half an hour early. It was a beautiful French bistro, tiny and charming, with big windows, a piano, and a thousand candles; the candlelight seemed to dapple to the music. This restaurant was about ten times nicer than any of the others we'd gone to, and it occurred to me that Josh must be very proud of a new poem.

He was so surprised that I was early that he lifted me off the ground to kiss me—or rather, I felt lifted off.

All through dinner, I could see how happy Josh was. We'd be talking, and then satisfaction would appear on his face and stay there: I imagined him thinking, *This steak is delicious, and also I think this is my best poem.*

He seemed so excited that I thought he might not wait until dessert to read his poem. But he did wait. We ate everything and sopped up the sauces with bread, so that our plates were shiny when we'd finished.

When the waitress cleared them, Josh asked her to wrap up our leftovers, and she smiled.

He held my hand and leaned over the table and kissed me. When he said, "You're so beautiful," I heard, *My poem is so beautiful.*

I was a little nervous, as I always was, that I wouldn't like his new poem or rather, that I wouldn't be able to pretend to love it.

"Well," I said, "are you going to read it to me?"

"Read what?" he said.

It was our six-month anniversary.

· · · · ·

I went to bed happy, but I woke up in the middle of the night. "What's the matter?" Josh said.

"I'm worried about my job," I said.

"Don't worry," he said.

I got up. I wandered around the dark, cavernous apartment and then went outside to the stairwell.

I smoked one cigarette, and then another.

I tried to pinpoint the problem. To myself, in the stairwell, I said, "Honey doesn't like me."

This brought back third grade, when I'd handed my father my report card and said, "Miss Snell doesn't like me." He'd said that my excuse disappointed him more than my grades.

Even though I knew that my father might be disappointed in me now, I also felt that he was the only one who could tell me what to do. But even wanting to call my father made me feel younger than I was supposed to be.

I tried to think of what he would say. It would be along the lines of, *Soon you'll find a job and get your own apartment.* What he said would be simple and even obvious, so I tried to think what the simple, obvious thing was.

I got it almost right away, along with the sensation that always came with my father's advice: *How could I not have known?*

I would have to work harder.

. . . . .

In the morning, when Josh asked if I wanted to go to the Met, I told him I needed to go in to the office. He went to the library for a bonus session of poetry writing.

At 375 Madison, I signed in with the guard in the lobby, and I saw that Francine Lawlor had signed in, too, at nine A.M.

She was sitting at her desk when I walked in, and, except for saying hello to me, she acted like it was a regular workday. From her waist up, it was: She had on a fluffy blouse and her orange-red jacket. When she stood, I saw that she was wearing jeans and sneakers—Wranglers cuffed over Keds.

I worked all day Saturday and went in again on Sunday. I made copies of a manuscript Honey wanted to hand out in Monday's editorial meeting; I typed all the letters she'd left for me on Friday. I made a neat pile of them, along with letters for the manuscripts to be rejected. I figured out what to do with everything in my TO FILE file; I recrumpled Jenny Ling's résumé and letter and threw them away.

I removed every piece of paper from my desk, and now I saw what was underneath: *20th-Century Typewriting*. I put it in a padded envelope and addressed it to the Surrey Free Library and left it in my OUT box.

Then I turned off my tensor lamp and said a fond farewell to Francine.

In the lobby, I signed out. The guard was doing a find-the-word puzzle in the newspaper. He was drawing what looked like a long worm around a word when I told him my name and asked for his. It was Warren. We shook hands.

It was dark outside, and cold. But the air felt good. I had worked hard and now it was over. I was tired and happy, a friend to guards and a worker in the workforce, and in the morning my boss would discover that even though I hadn't been the editor of the Yale literary magazine or received honors, honors, honors, even though I hadn't acquired a novel or edited two, I was the best editorial assistant in New York, and possibly the world.

6.

IT TOOK HONEY a few weeks to believe that my vast improvement was not a joke I was playing on her.

I went into the office every Saturday. At first, Francine and I hardly talked, except for hello and good-bye, and when I was going out I'd tell her what I was getting—a sandwich, a soda, a bagel—and ask if she wanted anything from the outside world; she never did.

Then, one Saturday, I asked her if she wanted coffee, and she said, "I just made a fresh pot."

I heard this as both an offer and a test; I said, "Do you mind if I have some?"

She said, "Of course not."

Our coffeemaker was just outside the conference room. During the week a pot was always on the burner, but only the truly desperate drank it. I poured myself a cupful and spooned in some nondairy powdered creamer.

Back at the Cave, I took a sip and tasted thousands of pots of coffee that had burned themselves into black bitterness; I tasted the burner itself.

After that first sip I sipped only for show, not letting the coffee enter my mouth; I smoked the peace pipe without inhaling.

It gave me the courage to ask Francine a question: "Where are you from?"

"Pennsylvania."

I said, "I'm from Pennsylvania," though usually I said that I was from Philadelphia, since Surrey was only a half-hour away.

"You're not from where I'm from," she said.

"Where are you from?"

She said, "You've never heard of it."

I waited.

"Lesher," she said.

I said, "I think I've heard of Lesher," though I hadn't. "Do your parents still live there?"

She seemed to be considering whether to answer me. "They're old."

"Oh." I didn't know what to say. "That's a drag."

. . . . .

For a while that's how it was: I'd ask Francine questions, and she'd grudgingly answer them. Where did she live? Carteret, New Jersey. Who was her favorite writer? Theodore Dreiser. Where had she gone to college? Ursinus.

It wasn't until the weekend after Bettina's promotion was announced that Francine talked. I came in late that Saturday afternoon, and she said, "I was wondering when you'd show up," the closest she had come to any familiarity. Was it a joke? In case it was, I smiled.

Once I was settled in, she said, "I can't believe Bettina got promoted."

"Yeah," I said. "Why?"

"Well, for one thing," she said, "her knowledge of punctuation begins and ends with her own beauty mark."

I laughed, and she did, too. I'd never heard her laugh before; it was a *k-k-k-k* sound, dry, like tiny twigs snapping.

. . . . .

"It's interesting to consider why an editor hires or promotes an assistant," she said one Saturday, handing me a cup of coffee from the pot she'd made.

"I know," I said, as though this was a thought I'd had myself.

"Mostly, it's narcissism," she said.

Then she was quiet, and I worried she was thinking about herself and why no editor had chosen her as a mirror. In case she was, I wanted to distract her. I said, "Why do you think Honey hired me?"

"I was just wondering about that," she said.

I hesitated before saying, "Honey used to go out with my brother."

Francine nodded. "That's perverse."

. . . . .

Francine rewrote the form letter that Steinhardt sent out with rejected slush manuscripts and asked me to proofread it for her.

"Is there anything you would change?"

I told her that signing "The Editors" above the typed "The Editors" looked a little strange to me.

"Strange?" she said, hating me for my word choice.

I tried to explain. "I mean 'the editors' is so anonymous I'm not sure you want to sign it."

She nodded, but her lips were still pursed from my *strange*.

I said, "Why don't you just sign your name?"

I could see she'd agonized over this question; it worried me how much thought she devoted to slush. "Then I'd have to use my title," she said.

"I think that's okay."

She said, "If I'd spent a decade writing a novel, I don't think I'd want to have it rejected by a floating assistant."

"Well," I said, "then the author could say, 'Yeah, well, what the fuck does she know? She's just a fucking floating assistant.' "

I was afraid I'd offended her with my *fuck* and *fucking*, but when I turned around she was smiling to herself. Maybe she liked the idea that her low status could serve a noble purpose.

* * * * *

I noticed that she was deep into a manuscript, and I asked her if it was good.

She said, "It is frightfully bad."

She appeared to be about four hundred pages in, so I said, "Why do you keep reading it?"

She said, "Every author deserves a chance."

* * * * *

I helped Francine push another carton of slush from the copier to her desk. As she pulled out the first manuscript, I saw her face: It was full of hope.

It hadn't occurred to me until that moment that Francine wanted anything more than what I wanted—not to get fired. But I'd been wrong: Francine was ambitious. She was looking for her promotion in those cartons.

She was no Honey and she knew it; she wasn't going to get a great manuscript messengered to her after a fancy lunch with a big-deal agent. No, Francine would have to read page after page, manuscript after manuscript, carton after carton to find the novel that would make her promotion indisputable.

It seemed impossible to me. I didn't think there was a publishable novel in any of those cartons, much less a great one. Even if there was, how could Francine ever find it, reading, as she did, all the pages of all those manuscripts?

I kept thinking that as her friend I should tell her so. In my head, I practiced speeches I would give her; they were gentle, full of praise but also reality.

* * * * *

Francine and I never talked in front of the other Cave-dwellers. The few times I tried, she just shook her head. I thought she was trying to protect me—maybe from Bettina—but it wasn't that. I think she wanted to distinguish herself from the rest of the assistants; I think she was trying to see herself as an editor whose paperwork had just been held up.

So I was surprised one Friday afternoon when I looked up from my typewriter, and she was standing above me.

"Would you read something for me?" she said. "For the editorial meeting on Monday?"

"Sure," I said, and I realized that she thought she'd found the slush novel that would transform her career. I told her that she should probably give the manuscript to some editors to read, too.

Francine hesitated.

I said, "Their support is going to mean a lot more than mine."

She didn't answer.

"That's what I'd do," I said.

Then I figured out what her hesitation was, and I said, "I can ask Honey if you want."

She said, "I'll make another copy."

· · · · ·

I caught Honey right before she left for the weekend. She was going to the country and had dressed for it. She wore a beautiful suede jacket and a full skirt and dark brown boots.

"I need a favor," I said.

She tilted her chin up at me.

I noticed that the novel was entitled *We* and its author named I. Tittlebaum, neither of which sounded too promising. I noticed, too, how heavy the manuscript was—i.e., long—and I realized what a big favor it was to ask Honey to read it over her weekend in the country.

When I repeated what I'd told Francine about Honey's opinion meaning more than mine, her expression said, *Obviously,* so I said, "Obviously."

"Sure," she said, "that's just how I want to spend my weekend." But she took it.

· · · · ·

We was about the principal of a high school in New Jersey the year his French-teacher wife leaves him and their children, and it was so great

I forgot that I was reading the novel as a favor. I read *We* all weekend and I was still reading it at 3 A.M. Sunday night.

Sometimes the editorial meeting started late or was postponed until the afternoon, and this was what I prayed for when I woke up at 9:45. I left the apartment without even brushing my teeth.

Not everyone looked up at me when I walked into the conference room; Honey didn't. Francine was sitting beside her at the table. I sat with the other assistants along the wall.

There was a huge stack of copies of *We* in front of Honey, and her Post-it note was still on top of the original. Without reading the note I knew it asked me to make however many copies were now beneath it.

The editors went clockwise around the table, talking about the novels and nonfiction they'd read and wanted to buy or pass on. Everyone tried to be fast, except one editor who liked to talk about all of her impressions.

Finally, it was Honey's turn. She began by just looking around the table until everyone was looking back at her. Then she said, "Francine Lawlor found this novel in the slush pile." I was relieved that she didn't call Francine "Clarisse."

Francine opened her mouth, and I thought she was going to take over but Honey went on.

Honey was a good saleswoman; she'd prepared an eloquent speech but made it sound like she was just talking to us. I noticed that while she compared I. Tittlebaum to the classic writers everyone admired, she compared *We* to books that had sold millions of copies.

She'd taken the liberty of calling I. Tittlebaum over the weekend to make sure that he hadn't sold the book to another publisher—he hadn't—and she went on to say what a wonderful man he was, and also that he was happy to change the book's title.

I was so captivated by her speech—everyone was—that at first I didn't notice the change in Francine's smile. It had been twitchy with excitement, but now it was frozen solid, and I understood why: Honey had made *We* her acquisition.

Honey apologized for the length of the novel; she said that she'd edit it down by a third.

This was the only shift I saw in Francine's expression; her eyes came to life for a second.

When Honey finished, she turned to Francine and said, "Is there anything you want to add?"

I admired the way Francine recovered. She tried to make her smile warm and said, "I hope you will all read this extraordinary novel."

I'd never spoken in an editorial meeting before, and it felt hard to now, especially without having brushed my teeth. But I wanted to do something to make *We* Francine's again.

I heard myself say, "Um," and saw heads at the table turn toward me.

Honey's look almost stopped me; it didn't show anything more than surprise, but it made me realize that she hadn't sanctioned my speaking in the meeting, which made whatever I said subversive.

Everyone was looking at me, waiting.

I thought of saying that Francine had read a thousand manuscripts to find this one, and that she'd read them with care and respect and all the way through. But I wasn't sure this was the speech I should give, and it was more than my mouth was capable of, anyway. "Francine asked me to read *We* over the weekend," I said. "And I loved it."

I could tell how slowly I'd said these words by how fast Honey cut me off: "Good," she said.

Then Francine passed out the manuscripts.

Back in the Cave, Bettina dropped hers on her desk and said, "Shit," at its heft.

Sue said, "Congratulations," to Francine, who said, "Thank you very much."

I went over to Francine and said, "I am so sorry."

Francine closed her eyes, and she kept them closed, and I knew suddenly that "I'm sorry" was the worst thing I could've said; she was trying to pretend that nothing bad had happened.

As fast as I could, I said, "I'm sorry you had to copy all those manuscripts instead of me."

She waited another minute to open her eyes and another to speak. "That's okay," she said. "I got the mail room to do it."

I wanted to ask if she'd seen Honey drop the manuscript off before the meeting, and if Honey had seemed mad that I hadn't been there. But it seemed wrong to worry about myself after what had happened to Francine, and I thought I'd find out soon, anyway.

I didn't, though. I didn't find out until Wednesday morning when I came in, and there was a message from Honey taped to the base of my tensor lamp.

The note said to call her, and I did.

She said, "Can you meet me in Wolfe's office?"

I said, "Sure."

. . . . .

Wolfe was sitting at his desk, and Honey stood at the window, too agitated to sit.

"Come on in," Wolfe said to me. "Have a seat."

I took the chair I'd sat in during my lunch with Wolfe.

He called Irene and asked her to hold his calls.

When Honey sat down next to me, I wanted to stand up and go to the sofa. But I stayed where I was.

She faced me, her hands clasped like Act One of the hand play *This Is the Church*.

As it turned out, Honey had gone to the Cave for the last three mornings and found my tensor lamp on, though I hadn't yet arrived. "It's the deception I mind," she said, and her voice was so angry that it trembled a little; for the first time it occurred to me that some of what she felt for me might belong to Jack.

I said, "I never asked anyone to turn my lamp on."

I worried that Francine would get in trouble because of me, but Honey moved on. Apparently it was not only the deception she minded. She went on about my lateness and the warning she'd given me and my promise to come in earlier.

She was building her case.

I looked at Wolfe: *Save me.*

But he was looking at Honey. In his face I saw that this meeting was distasteful to him.

He got up and went to the stereo. He spent a minute looking through his records, and I saw Honey roll her eyes. I realized that she didn't like Wolfe.

I wondered if he liked her. I hoped he didn't, but I knew it didn't matter. He was fair, like my father; even if Wolfe liked me more than he liked Honey, he would be on the side of the argument that was right, no matter whose it was. This was the way you were supposed to be at work, and it probably deepened my respect for him, though I couldn't feel that yet. What I felt was that he was not going to protect or defend me.

He put on *Kind of Blue.* I took this as a message from him to me, though I wasn't sure what it meant.

When he sat down again, he nodded at me.

"I *am* late almost every day," I said. "But I stay late to make up for it."

Wolfe's expression relaxed a little.

"I come in every weekend," I said.

No one spoke or moved for a minute.

Then Honey plopped down on the sofa as an adolescent might. This seemed to strengthen my case.

"Okay," Wolfe said to me, my signal to go. "Thanks."

I felt I'd won for the moment, if only in the impartial court of Judge Wolfe. For the first time in my life, I'd done my homework, and it made me feel strong and hardworking and virtuous, as I never had before; I felt impervious.

This lasted about thirty seconds, until I got back to the Cave and realized what I'd done. Even if I'd won with Wolfe, I'd lost and lost big with Honey. I'd made my own boss look bad in front of hers, and it occurred to me that I was now in roughly double the trouble of lateness and deception, and I didn't know what punishment might come next.

Still, I didn't feel scared. I felt calm. I felt like I was beginning to understand something.

Across from me, Francine was reading a manuscript. She was more virtuous than I would ever be, she had done more homework than I would ever do, and here she was, buried in slush.

Adam, the embodiment of discretion, called me on the phone.

"Are you okay?" he said.

I told him that I was alive and unfired.

. . . . .

I. Tittlebaum drove in from New Jersey later that week.

Honey called and asked me to come down to her office to meet him. "Bring Clarisse," she said.

I said, "Francine."

Francine looked up at me.

I. Tittlebaum was taller than his name seemed to suggest, and much younger than the character in his novel. He couldn't possibly have teenaged children, and if his wife had left him, she'd come back or he'd found somebody else; he wore a wedding band.

Wolfe nodded at Francine and me, but he let Honey make the introductions. She said, "Irv, I want you to meet the assistant who found your book in the slush pile: Francine Lawlor."

For some reason, he reached out to shake my hand.

"No," I said, and my voice was louder than it should've been, because his thinking I was Francine, or wanting me to be, added insult to the injury of her not getting her due.

Honey's expression didn't change, though I was pretty sure she thought my faux pas had ruined her faux tribute.

"This is Francine," I said, though she was already shaking hands with the author.

She said, "It's a wonderful book, Mr. Tittlebaum."

He said, "Thank you," and in it you could hear that he was thanking her for everything, thanking her for more than Honey would've liked.

He stood there gazing at Francine until Honey nabbed the attention back. "And this is my assistant, Sophie Applebaum," she said, pronouncing my name like it was an important one for him to know.

I said, "Hi."

Wolfe said, "Francine, will you join us for lunch?"

"Thank you," she said, "but I have work to do."

. . . . .

Francine and I walked down the hall back to the Cave without talking. She stopped at her desk, but I knew that if I were in her place, I would need to cry—I felt like crying in my own place—so I said, "Come on," and led her out the back door and past the restrooms. Her eyes widened a little when I opened the door to the smoking balcony.

"I'm surprised it isn't locked," she said.

I said, "I know."

The sky was cloudy, with a pale sun. It was almost spring. I'd never seen Francine in natural light, and in the sun I saw now that her hair was more white than blond.

We were both looking out at the buildings, though there wasn't really anything to see. I was trying to think of something reassuring to say to her; I was trying to think of what I'd want someone to say to me.

But when I looked over, her face wasn't sad. If anything, she looked serene. Maybe she was remembering the grateful look I. Tittlebaum had given her. She might have just felt glad that she'd done her job well and found a good book for Steinhardt to publish. Or maybe she knew that in a few weeks Wolfe would promote her.

Whatever it was, I was relieved that she wasn't upset. It made me feel less guilty about giving *We* to Honey.

I took my pack of cigarettes out and offered one to her almost as a joke, but she took it. I lit it for her.

I thought she'd just hold it and take non-inhaling puffs like my grandmother, but she smoked like a smoker.

"You smoke?" I said.

"Yes," she said.

This cheered me up a little. It made me think that there might be other things I didn't know about this talented editor, Dreiser lover, Ursinus alumna, and citizen of Carteret, New Jersey. I hoped there were.

RUN RUN RUN RUN RUN
RUN RUN RUN AWAY

WHEN MY BROTHER tells me he's been seeing a psychiatrist, I say, "That's great, Jack."

He says, "What—you think I'm fucked up?"

I say, "How'd you find him?"

He says, "What makes you think my psychiatrist is a man?"

Her name is Mary Pat Delmar, and Jack tells me she is brilliant. He says, "She blows me away," and I think they must be talking a lot about junior high.

"Wow," I say.

He smiles. "I told her you'd say that."

When he tells me how beautiful she is, I say, "But not so beautiful that you have trouble concentrating?"

"She's pretty beautiful," he says. Plus impressive: She won a scholarship to college, for example, and put herself through medical school; she grew up in rural Tennessee, where her parents still run a luncheonette.

I say, "She told you all that?"

"Yeah," he says. "Why?"

"I don't think of psychiatrists talking that much."

It's not until he tells me that they're not in Freudian analysis and breaks out laughing that I realize he's not in analysis at all. Mary Pat is his new girlfriend.

He laughs like a madman, and I say, "Very funny," though it is, in fact, very funny just to hear Jack laugh, as well as a huge relief: Our father died not even two months ago.

My eggs and Jack's pancakes are set before us, and we stop talking to eat; we're at Homer's, the diner around the corner from his apartment in the Village.

I ask how he met Mary Pat.

He tells me, "Pete referred her."

For a moment he gets waylaid talking about the fishing shack he helped Pete restore this summer. Pete lives year-round on Martha's Vineyard with his Newfoundland, Lila, who expresses her heartache by howling to Billie Holiday records: *Dog, you don't know the trouble I seen.*

Jack says Pete called when M.P. moved to town. "I think he's always been a little in love with her."

I say nothing; I have always been a little in love with Pete.

· · · · ·

Though Jack didn't say he'd bring Mary Pat, I'm a little disappointed when he arrives at Homer's without her. "Just coffee," he says to the waiter.

He tells me that M.P. was mugged on her way home from work, and he was up half the night trying to calm her down.

"Jesus," I say, and ask where and when, and was there a weapon?

A knife; ten P.M.; a block from her apartment on Avenue D.

I say, "She lives on Avenue D?" D is for Drugs, D is for Danger, D is for Don't live on Avenue D unless you have to.

Jack says, "It's what she can afford."

"I thought psychiatrists cleaned up."

"Maybe in private practice," he says.

As Dr. Delmar, Mary Pat treats survivors of torture in a program at NYU Hospital.

From spending weeks at my father's bedside I have become alive to a level of pain I'd never known: Now I feel it on every street of Manhattan, in every column in the newspaper, and just the idea of someone who works to ease suffering eases mine.

I say, "When can I meet her?"

"Soon."

Sounding like a worried mother, I say, "She should take a cab when she works late."

"She says walking is her only exercise."

. . . . .

When I arrive at the White Horse, Jack says, "Want to sit outside?"

It's November. "Why would I want to sit outside?"

He tells me that M.P. will; after spending all day in the hospital, she craves fresh air. He takes off his leather jacket and hands it to me, an act of chivalry in the name of Mary Pat.

I give in. "You love this girl."

He howls a mock-forlorn, "I do," imitating a country singer or Newfoundland.

We maneuver our legs under a picnic table; we are the sole outsiders, and Jack has to go inside to get the waitress.

We both order scotch for warmth.

Jack yawns and tells me that he and Mary Pat were up most of the night, discussing his new screenplay. He tells me that her notes are incredibly smart, unbelievably smart—smarter than his actual screenplay.

It occurs to me that I have never heard him more sure of any woman and less sure of himself.

He catches sight of his dramaturge across the street, and I turn to look.

She is tall and skinny in high heels. She has long, wavy hair. Her cheeks are flushed, and when she sees Jack she smiles, activating dimples.

Her hand is limp in mine, her voice shivery as she says, "Pleased to meet you."

She kisses Jack full on the mouth and then says she thinks she's coming down with something; do we mind sitting inside?

Once we're seated, I pretend, as I always do with Jack's girlfriends, that I already like her: I tell her that I can hardly sit in high heels, let alone walk in them, and how does she do it?

"I don't know," she says.

Jack puts his hand across her forehead, and his eyebrows slant up in worry. "You have a fever."

"If you're sick," I say, "we can have dinner another night."

"No, no," she says. "I like a fever." Her smile is wan, her skin shiny. "You know, through the glass darkly."

I do not know; I'm not even sure I've heard her correctly. Her voice is so quiet I strain just for fragments.

We pick up our menus.

"I'm going to have a cheeseburger and fries," I say.

Jack says, "Same here."

Mary Pat says, "I don't think I can eat a whole one myself."

"You can share mine," he says.

"You don't mind?"

My brother, who usually slaps my hand if I take one of his fries, does not mind.

When our burgers arrive, Mary Pat ignores the extra plate brought for sharing and eats right off Jack's. Instead of cutting the cheeseburger in half, she takes a bite, and then he does. She even uses his napkin to wipe her mouth. I am reminded of the aid organization Doctors Without Borders.

"Jack told me that you met through Pete," I say.

"Oh, yes." She says, "He warned your brother about me," and the two of them seem to think this is funny.

I play along—ha, ha, ha: "What did he say?"

Jack asks Mary Pat, "What did he say?"

She says, "I'm trouble?" her voice so lush with sex, I think, *Hey, M.P., I'm right here, Jack's little sister, across the table.*

Her body reacts to the smallest shift in his; they are in constant bodily contact. She doesn't touch Jack directly, but rubs herself against him almost incidentally, like a cat. The one time he reaches for her hand, she lets him hold it for less than a minute; then she takes it back and hides it in the dark under the table.

Maybe because of her whispery voice or her ethereal skinniness or her glass-darkly fever, Mary Pat gives the impression of not quite being here at the table, here at the White Horse, here on Earth. To assure myself of my own existence, I counter her quiet voice by raising mine, counter her little bites by taking big ones.

I try to talk to her, but it is just me asking questions and her answering them. My questions get longer, her answers shorter. Still I don't quit. I'm like a gambler who keeps thinking, *Maybe the next hand.*

The name of her parents' luncheonette? Delmar's.

The division of labor? Her father cooks; her mother serves.

If we were at Delmar's now, we'd order . . . ? "Meat 'n' Two."

I say, "Meat and two?"

"One meat and two sides."

I love sides; I ask which are best.

"Butter beans," she says. "Grits, if you like grits."

I nod the nod of a grits liker, though not a single grit has ever entered my mouth. I say, "Did you hang out at the luncheonette a lot growing up?"

"Yes."

I say, "Was it fun?"

"No," she says, making clear that she doesn't want to talk about this or to talk to me or to talk. She says, "Excuse me," and goes to the ladies' room.

"What?" I say to Jack.

He says, "She can't talk about her father."

"Were we talking about her father?"

When she returns, Jack puts his arm around her.

I say, "I didn't mean to pry."

Mary Pat says a wounded, "Don't worry about it."

· · · · ·

Jack does not call to ask what I think of Mary Pat, as he has with every other girlfriend he has ever introduced to me. He doesn't call at all.

When I call him, he is in bed with a fever of 103.

I offer to bring him soup, and he says that he has soup and juice and everything he needs—left over from when he took care of Mary Pat.

. . . . .

A week later, when I call to ask if we're meeting at Homer's, he's still in bed.

He says that his fever is down; he just doesn't feel good.

I say, "What's the matter, Buddy?" our father's nickname for Jack.

"She hated my revision."

"What?"

"I told you she gave me notes on my script," he says. "She said I didn't understand anything."

I say, "You want me to come over?"

"Yeah," he says, and I go.

His night table is a mess of drugs—NyQuil, DayQuil, Sudafed, Theraflu—a sticky dose cup, a mug, and a tea bag that looks like a mouse in rigor mortis. His bed is covered with screenplay pages and used Kleenexes, which, he says, are of equal value to Mary Pat.

"Does she know that your father died nine weeks ago?"

He says, "I asked her to be honest."

It takes me a minute to understand that he is defending her against me.

I clean up, I take his temperature, I make tea. I am stirring soup when Mary Pat calls, apparently contrite.

"She's coming over," Jack says, which means I'm supposed to go.

. . . . .

Jack arrives at Homer's, blurry with exhaustion and hobbling. He tells me that he's been working out. "I just overdid it." He says something indecipherable through a yawn, and, ". . . up really late."

I ask if he was working on his screenplay.

"No." He yawns. "No."

I yawn.

"We stayed up late, talking," he says.

"Do you babies ever sleep through the night?"

He says, "She was upset."

I think of the work that Mary Pat does and the stories she must hear every day.

"I woke up," Jack says, "and she was crying."

I nod in sympathy.

His voice is cloudy with sleep. "She kept telling me how sorry she was."

I say, "Why was she sorry?"

He seems suddenly to focus, and to realize that he might not want to tell me this story. He hesitates before going on, but he does go on, too tired to obey his instincts. "She's still in love with her old boyfriend."

The words seem to spell out *The End,* and yet I don't hear *The End* in his voice or see *The End* in his face.

I say, "If she loves him so much, how come she broke up with him?"

I watch Jack try to remember. "She didn't feel she deserved to be happy back then."

What comes to mind is Jack's rendition of the Talking Heads' song he changed from "Psycho Killer" to "Psycho Babble," and the refrain, "Run run run run run run run away."

I say, "When didn't she deserve to be happy?"

"Her freshman year," he says. "He was a senior. Physics major. He played squash."

I'm confused. "So, she's been seeing him since her freshman year?"

"No," he says.

"She ran into him?"

"No."

"But she wants to get back together with him?"

"No," he says. "He's married with two kids. She doesn't even know where he lives."

It occurs to me that I might understand this story better if I were really, really tired.

My poor brother's eyes are tiny and his skin clam-colored; his hand trembles as he returns his coffee cup to the puddle in his saucer. He says, "The good thing is . . ." and drifts off.

I say, "The good thing is . . ."

"She finally feels like she deserves to be happy."

. . . . .

Jack calls and says that he wishes he hadn't told me about M.P.'s old boyfriend.

I say, "I understand," and I do. There are things that two people say in the middle of the night that don't make sense to a third at breakfast.

. . . . .

The next few times I ask, Jack tells me that Mary Pat is great, and then she is good, and then she is fine, and then she is okay.

Saturday night, at four A.M., he calls me from her apartment. I know without asking that he is sitting in the dark; I can hear it in his voice.

"I blew it," he says.

I say, "I'm sure you didn't."

"I did," he says. "I blew it."

"How?"

"I just blew it," he says. "I blew it."

"Try to remember that we're having a conversation," I say, "and your goal is to impart information."

He says, "I should've proposed to her at the Boathouse."

When I don't answer, he says, "In Central Park," as though to clarify. "That was the perfect moment."

I force myself to say the consoling words: "I'm sure you'll have another perfect moment."

"No," he says. "She said that was the perfect moment, and we can never get it back."

"Hold on there," I say. "You've known each other for, like, twenty minutes."

He doesn't answer, and I hear how irrelevant these words are to him. I'm worried that he's going to hang up and propose now. "Just bear with me," I say. "Forget about perfect moments for a minute. Do you really want *Mary Pat* to be your *wife*? You want *Mary Pat* to be the *mother of your children*?"

"Yes," he says.

I do not ask him if he thinks he would be happy with Mary Pat. Happiness, I realize, is beside the point. I realize, too, that he doesn't want to figure anything out or to feel better. He wants me to help him win Mary Pat.

"Okay," I say. "Here's what I think you should do. Don't ask her to marry you. Give her room. Try not to need anything from her for a little while."

How can I tell that I have said something he wants to hear? The silence is just the same, but I know.

I imitate our father's calm authority: "We'll figure the rest out in the morning."

· · · · ·

I've only called Pete a few times in my life, and as soon as I hear his hello, I remember why. He has settled in for the night, his feet by the fire, Dostoyevsky in hand, Lila's head on his lap; a phone call is breaking and entering.

We talk, but only about one percent of Pete comes to the phone. You get close to Pete by swimming or clamming or fishing, by weeding his garden or singing while he plays guitar.

Every exchange is more strained than the last until I get to the emergency of my brother's love. When I finish, Pete says, "I don't think there's anything you can do, Soph." He is sympathetic but resolute; I imagine this is the voice he uses to tell clients a house is beyond restoration.

"You don't understand," I say. "I think he's going to propose to her."

"They all propose," he says.

For myself, I say, "Did you propose?"

He laughs. "No." It occurs to me that I have never known Pete to have a girlfriend.

I say, "How are you?"

"You know," he says. "Okay."

"How's Lila?"

He says, "How are you, Lila?"

What I hear in the moment of quiet that follows is Martha's Vineyard in winter—the clouds in the sky, the wind on the beach, and the cold that stays on your clothes even inside.

· · · · ·

Jack does not return my calls. I ask my mother if she's heard from him. She has. She says, "I can't wait to meet Mary Pat."

· · · · ·

I know how hard my little brother is working, and I am reluctant to worry him. But when he asks me what I think of Mary Pat, I tell him everything. "He's losing weight," I say. "He doesn't sleep anymore." It occurs to me that this is how cults weaken the will of initiates.

Robert says, "It sounds like he's in love," and adds that the world's most coveted state is characterized by unrelieved insecurity and almost constant pain.

The effect of his words is to remind me that it has been a long time since I have been in love.

"What about you?" Robert says. "Have you met anyone?"

He always asks, and I always have to say no, and I say no now. For the first time, he says he wants to introduce me to someone he knows, a pediatric heart surgeon.

"That's good," I say. "I have a pediatric heart."

He says, "Don't talk about my sister that way."

Before we hang up, I say, "Are you in love?"

"No," he says.

I ask if his wife knows.

"Of course," he says. "Naomi's the one who told me."

· · · · ·

When Jack finally calls me, at work, he says, "Can you meet me?" instead of *Hello*.

I say, "When?"

He says, "Now."

Before I can ask where, he hangs up.

Even though it's six P.M. on a weekday, I assume Homer's, and I'm right. Jack's at the counter, his head bowed.

His face looks haggard, but his body is surprisingly buff.

He says that he can't sleep or eat or think or write.

"Apparently you can work out, though," I say.

"She won't call me back," he says.

"I know how that feels."

He misses the jibe. "We had a fight," he says.

"About what?"

"It wasn't really a fight." He tells the waiter, "Just coffee."

"He'll have pancakes and bacon with that." To Jack, I say, "Or do you want eggs?"

"I don't want anything," he says.

I tell the waiter, "He'll have the pancakes."

Jack doesn't even seem to hear.

"You seem like you're in a coma," I say, and as soon as I say it, I feel sick. Our father was in a coma for days, and I have said *coma* the way people who don't know anything about it do, which is like calling out, *Can we get another coma over here?*

I say, "I meant stupor," but Jack is in such a stupor, he didn't even notice my *coma*.

When his pancakes come, he pushes the plate aside. He sighs, and sighs again. His voice is so quiet, it's as though he's talking to himself when he says, "I can't hit her."

"Sorry?"

"I can't hit her," he says, and I realize how tired and desperate he must be to say these words to me.

"And you want to hit her?"

He shrugs. "She wants me to."

"In bed," I say.

"Of course in bed," he says. "Where else?"

"Oh, I'm sorry," I say. "Of course, she wants you to hit her in bed. And you can't. Go on."

"She thinks it means I don't love her."

I say, "Can I hit her?"

"Sophie." His voice is a reprimand. "Her father used to beat her."

I think, *She probably deserved it,* but then I turn back into a human being.

My brother's face is so tired and so sad it makes my face tired and sad. "Buddy." But even as I say, "If I were you, I'd try to get out of this thing," I know that nothing I say, no matter how wise or well put, will separate him from this woman.

"It's not like I have a choice," he says.

I say, "Of course you do."

"She's been seeing someone else," he says. "Some guy she works with."

I am about to say, *A victim?* but I correct myself in time: "A survivor?"

He defends Mary Pat even now: "She would never go out with a patient."

There are so many things I could say about Mary Pat. I could call her the one word you save for occasions such as this, the only sacred profanity. But my brother loves this woman, whoever she is, and deriding her would only deride him for loving her.

What else is there to say? I tell him that I've been editing a celebrity diet book at work. I say, "News flash: Eat less, exercise more."

When I slide the plate of pancakes in front of him, he says, "I'm not hungry."

"Do you think I care if you're hungry?" I say. "This has nothing to do with hunger. Hunger is beside the point. Hunger is a luxury you can't afford."

I pour syrup over the pancakes. When I cut into the stack, he says, drily, "Leggo my Eggo," repeating a commercial circa our childhood.

"You need a nap," I say.

He eats one bite, and then another.

While he finishes his pancakes, I plan the future. I will walk him home, and up the stairs to his apartment. He'll lie down. I'll shop for groceries. I will take him to a movie and out to dinner. In case my father is listening, I think, *We will look after each other.*

DENA BLUMENTHAL +
BOBBY ORR FORREVER

My MOTHER is at her bereavement group, and I am on the phone with a distant relative I don't know, an ancient guiltress, who says she's sorry about my father but turns out to be a lot sorrier that no one bothered to let her know at the time, so she could've come to his funeral. She keeps saying things like, "Is it so hard to pick up the phone and dial?"

I am saved by the beep of Call Waiting and ask her to hold on a minute, please. She says, "This is long distance."

A second beep. "Well, nice talking to you," I say, and, "I'll give my mother your message," though I don't think I will. "Good-bye."

The other call is Dena, and I launch into an instant replay of the guilt festival I've just attended, which fascinates me now that it's over, but not Dena. I hear indulgence in her, "Uh-huh."

I say, "She didn't even know my name. It was like the guilt equivalent of anonymous sex—"

Dena says, "How are you?"

She is asking big, but I answer little: "Fine," I say. "How are you?"

This she treats as a digression, as though I am a patient inquiring after my doctor's health. She allows only a few questions about her life before switching back to mine. "Have you talked to Demetri?"

I haven't.

"Good," she says. "When are you coming back to New York?"

I make my voice casual: "I don't know."

I expect her to laugh when I tell her that I have an interview at *Shalom*, the newsletter we grew up not reading.

She doesn't say anything.

I wait and then say, "I should get ready," even though my interview isn't for another three hours.

She says, "Bob," her nickname for me and mine for her since high school, "you're living in Surrey," and she says these words with the sympathetic authority of one familiar with Surrey's social opportunities—the kids smoking cigarettes outside the skating rink; the housewife returning a nylon nightie at Strawbridge & Clothier; the mustached neighbor walking a miniature schnauzer named Pepper.

I say, "The good thing about being nowhere in your career is that you can do it anywhere."

She says, "Bob."

"Yeah?"

She hesitates. "Good luck."

. . . . .

I'd only been with Demetri for a few months when he asked me to go to Los Angeles with him.

"Come with me," he said, and my heart stopped hurting for the first time since my father's death.

I was thrilled quitting my job, thrilled giving up my apartment. It seemed like the first real risk I'd ever taken. I felt like I was kissing life right on the lips.

I started to panic the week before we were supposed to leave. Suddenly I heard everything everybody had been saying and not saying about Demetri: Dena had called him a pathological narcissist; my older brother had said, "There's no there there"; my younger brother had sighed.

But it was the idea of my father that I couldn't shake. I knew what he would've thought of Demetri—not that he would've said so. He would've said, *What are you going to do in Los Angeles?*

"What am I going to do in Los Angeles?" I said to Demetri.

He didn't know I was saying the *Dear* of Dear John. He told me I would spend my days fantasizing about the sex we'd have that night, and then that night we'd have it.

. . . . .

All my life, I've seen *Shalom* on our mail table, and now that I want to read it, it's gone. My mother threw it away, and the garbage men have come and gone. Everyone she calls has thrown theirs out, too. She's sure she saved the issues announcing my brothers' bar mitzvahs: We spend the hour before my interview fruitlessly rummaging through drawers stuffed with the memorabilia of childhood—sponge paintings of snowmen, compositions with sentences like, "The bird hops across the lawn."

My mother feels terrible about throwing out *Shalom* and insists on driving me to my interview. Lately, she's been giving me career pep talks, though she herself has not held a job since before my thirty-three-year-old brother was born. If I'm interested in journalism, she says now, *Shalom* is as good a place as any to start. "It's all about networking," she says. "And expanding your skill set."

"Well," I say, "you would know."

She starts to apologize, and I stop her. I tell her that I know she's trying to help, though her advice seems to be cutting off the air supply in the car and that's giving me brain damage.

I change the topic: Does she know Elaine Brodsky, the publisher I'm about to meet?

When she says, "I've known Elaine forever," her voice boards the *Mayflower*, a bad sign.

"Are you friends?" I say.

She says, "We're not close," her way of saying she dislikes a person. I hope it's one-way; my first boss was a disgruntled ex-girlfriend of my older brother.

We park in the lot for the Professional Offices at Manor, a concrete box with windows tinted brown like sunglasses. My mother says she'll wait for me; she's brought an old *New Yorker* to read, as she did during my violin lessons in high school.

As I get out of the car, she wishes me good luck and says, "You'll be fabulous."

The walkway is encrusted with ice; even in low heels I'm slow and

unsteady, a toddler learning to walk, an old woman afraid of breaking a hip.

A moment after the receptionist announces my arrival, out comes Elaine Brodsky in an inexplicably familiar kilt with an oversized gold-tone safety pin.

In her office, she says, "How's Mother?" Her voice isn't as cold as my mother's, but it isn't warm. She says, "I was so sorry to hear about Dad," like we're all one big unhappy family.

She's somber for a respectful moment before launching into the exciting happenings at *Shalom*.

I try to mirror her enthusiasm for their new volunteer staff—a cub reporter from the Hebrew school and a secretary from the Jewish Home for the Aged: "Wow."

She says, "We're helping each other." Then she turns the topic to me: She just loves my publishing background! Do I like to write? That'll certainly come in handy, as I'll be doing most of the reporting myself.

It is possibly the best interview I've ever had. I can tell she's going to offer me the job. In a few minutes I will again be one with the working world.

She wants me to meet *Shalom*'s current editor. After she dials his extension, she hands me the most recent issue of "The Weekly Newsletter Serving the Jewish Community of Greater Philadelphia" and she says, "Hot off the press."

I read the headline of the lead story: MRS. JACOBY'S FIFTH-GRADE CLASS LIGHTS THE HANUKKAH MENORAH.

The fifth grader in me knows that however desperate I am to get a job I am more desperate not to have this one, and once Elaine is off the phone, out of my mouth these words come: "I don't know anything about Judaism—is that a big part of the job?"

I'm as stunned as she is. The man who would have been my predecessor walks in and we shake hands, and then Elaine Brodsky is saying, "Give my best to Mother."

Mother and I drive home.

I'm lying on my bed when I spot Elaine Brodsky's kilt on Molly,

the doll my grandmother Steeny brought back from Scotland for me. Molly sits on a shelf along with Gigi from France, Frieda from Germany, and Erin from Ireland, each dressed in her country's native costume. I haven't noticed the dolls for a long time, and now that I do, they seem to sing, "It's a small world after all," about mine.

When my mother calls, "It's Dena," I pick up the phone.

She says, "How was it?"

"Great," I say. "Amazing." Then I tell her.

She laughs, and tries to make me see how hilarious the interview was. I do for about one second. Then I remember I am living at home with my mother in Surrey, and I will be living here forever. Lying on my canopy bed, looking at my costumed dollies, talking on my Princess phone, I can feel myself aging at an accelerated rate. Soon people will mistake my mother and me for sisters.

Dena says, "You need to get out of the house."

"Where should I go," I say, "the drugstore?"

"Go downtown and see a movie," she says. "Go to my house." She likes this idea so much she repeats it, and now it's an order: "Go to my house." She tells me she's calling her mother as soon as we hang up.

Recently Dena started liking her mother, or at least seeing why someone else might.

"I'm calling her right now," she says.

· · · · ·

The Blumenthals live in the only real mansion in Surrey, the house all other houses aspire to. It's old and vine-covered, with a pool hidden in back. There's a big formal living room no one uses, and the dining room ditto, but there are also rooms that seem private and warm—a little alcove with a window seat, Mrs. Blumenthal's dressing room with its deco vanity, and the library with its fireplace.

Growing up I envied their kitchen most, which had anything and everything you could want—white-papered packages of cold cuts, fresh rye bread, and bagels from the delicatessen, Coke and Tab and Sprite, Doritos and Fritos, Mallomars and Oreos, ice-cream cones covered with a helmet of chocolate and nuts, and at least two flavors of Häagen-Dazs, usually chocolate chocolate chip and butter pecan; if what you wanted wasn't in the kitchen, it was in the butler's pantry. I'd go home comparing their staples to ours—leftover chicken, celery, and vanilla ice milk.

The Blumenthals' housekeeper did the shopping, cleaning, and what little cooking there was. Her name was Flossie, and everyone seemed to like her better than they liked each other.

Dena's sisters, Tracy and Ellen, identical twins were both gymnasts and both cheerleaders. Dena called Ellen shallow and Tracy witchy, but they were indistinguishably fascinating to me. When the three sisters found themselves together, always by accident—to watch television or sit by the pool—the mood was reluctant forbearance.

Their father occasionally announced that he wanted them to behave like a real family, and he would suddenly decide that they were all going to Florida to play tennis or to Utah to ski; he'd insist that they were going to sit down as a family for dinner, though he himself would be the one missing the next evening.

In a pearl-gray cashmere sweater large enough to fit over his belly, Dr. Blumenthal gave the impression of being expert at his own comfort. I don't think I ever saw him without a drink in his hand—a beer after tennis, a gin and tonic by the pool, a martini in the evening, a Bloody Mary on Sunday, and so on. He could be convivial or blustery—often convivial then blustery.

Mrs. Blumenthal seemed immune to both. Taller than her husband and lithe, she carried herself like the great tennis player she was. Her hair was long for a mother, frosted a color Dena called "Surrey blond," and with her regal demeanor made her look a lot like her Russian wolfhounds before they got old.

She was always reading in a big armchair by the fire or on the white divan in her pristine bedroom, with a cup of tea or a glass of wine and an ashtray on the table beside her. She'd ask me if I was reading anything I loved, and if I was, she'd write down the title.

This afternoon when she opens the door, she's holding her place in *Madame Bovary*. She kisses me on both cheeks and says, "Sophie"; she has a throaty, smoker's voice.

"Hi," I say. She's asked me to call her Stevie—short for Stephanie—but I can't bring myself to call her anything but Mrs. Blumenthal, so I avoid calling her anything.

As I follow her into the library, she says, "What can I get you to drink?"

I ask what she's having.

"I haven't started yet."

I say, "What would you drink if . . ." I try to think of a crisis that would make her feel as bad as I feel now. "If Dr. Blumenthal said he was leaving you?"

"Champagne," she says, deadpan. Then: "I think we're in a brown mood—scotch, bourbon . . ."

"Bourbon," I say, though I can't tell the difference.

We sit in the big armchairs by the fire, and she lights a cigarette for herself and one for me. "Let's talk about money," she says.

"Okay."

She says, "Are you in debt, Sophie?"

"No."

"Good." Then: "I'm assuming your father left you something."

"He did."

She asks how much, and I tell her. I can't tell whether she thinks it's a little or a lot. "And how much would it cost you to move back to New York?"

"I don't know."

"Well," she says, "think about it."

I tell her that my father specifically asked me not to use the inheritance for living expenses; he wanted me to use it toward a down payment on a house or for a trip—something momentous.

"That's a nice idea." She pauses. "But you could always pay it back, once you're working."

I want to be closer to the fire, and I slide off my chair to the rug, where the wolfhounds once lounged. I wonder if Mrs. Blumenthal misses them.

She says, "Maybe we should talk about why you're in Surrey."

I try to think of the dogs' names: *Masha and Ivan?*

"I don't know whether you're trying to go back to a time before your father died," she says, "or whether you can't bring yourself to move on."

It's both—though I realize it only now.

"You just don't have the energy it takes?" she says.

I nod.

She says, "I've felt that way."

I'm amazed that she's speaking so honestly about her life. No one my mother's age ever does, or at least not to me.

I'm warm by the fire, but it's gotten dark outside; looking at the black windowpanes, I can feel the cold. The house seems quiet and still. I wonder if Dr. Blumenthal is home more or less now that all the girls are gone. I wonder if he is on his way home now, and if Mrs. Blumenthal herself knows. My father always called before leaving the courthouse to ask if my mother needed him to pick up anything, even though in all those years she never did.

It occurs to me that maybe Mrs. Blumenthal wasn't kidding about the champagne.

She says, "What about this boyfriend of yours in Los Angeles?"

I wonder what Dena has said. "Ex-boyfriend," I say. "Demetri."

"What does he do?"

I say that he writes for a sitcom now, but he's a comic. For some reason I think she may think he's a clown, so I say, "You know, he does stand-up—"

"Thanks," she says. "I know what a comic is. Is he funny?"

I say that he is. Onstage he does shticks, like the one about his role on a soap opera: "I'm not an actor, but I play one on TV." But alone with me he could be hilarious. I consider imitating his imitation of what his pets would say if they could talk. But thinking of Demetri at his funniest makes me miss him.

I hear myself say, "I keep expecting him to call." I haven't admitted this to anyone, and it's a relief to say it out loud. Still, I don't say the whole truth: I've been hoping he'll call and say how much he misses

Seth says the name of the band, and I can tell Vincent's impressed and doesn't want to be; he fast-talks about starting up a start-up—an online recording studio, a real-time distribution outlet, a virtual music label. He goes on and on, Vincent style, grandiose and impossible to understand.

I say, "Basically, you do everything but teach kindergarten?"

Vincent says, "There is an educational component."

Seth squeezes my hand three times.

"Oh, shoot," I say, looking at my wrist for a watch I'm not wearing, "we have to go," and I love the sound of *we*, and I love that it's Seth who wants to go, and I love that we are going.

Vincent says they're headed to another party themselves. He kisses both my cheeks—what now must be the signature Enzo kiss—and he looks at me as though he cares deeply for me, a look I never got when we were together, a look that Seth notices, and I think, *Phew! Seth will think another man loved me; he will think I am the lovable kind of woman, the kind a man better love right or somebody else will.*

Vincent says, "You look great, Sophie," and I think of saying, *Whereas you look a little strange,* but I just say, "See you, Vinnie."

A few more pleasantries, and Seth and I are on the elevator, just the two of us, pressing 1.

I say, "Good thing she was just a model." I am giddy, talking fast, and happy. "I think that would've been really hard if she were a super-model."

Seth looks at me, not sure what I mean.

Out on the street, I say, "How do you know her, by the way?" and instantly regret how deliberately offhanded I sound.

"I don't really know her," he says. "She came up to me after a show a few weeks ago."

I think, *Came* up *to you or* on *to you?* but I give myself the open, amused look of a bystander eager to hear more about one of life's funny little coincidences.

"She asked me if I would help her celebrate her half-birthday," he says, and his tone tells me I would be crazy to think he'd ever be interested in her.

Unfortunately, now I am crazy, and I have to stop myself from saying a tone-deaf and tone-dumb, *So you're saying you didn't eat her half-birthday cake?*

Suddenly I feel like I'm Mary Poppins, floating with an umbrella and a spoonful of sugar into the city of sexual menace, population a million models with ultra-short and long straight hair and pouty mouths and thighs you can see through mesh stockings.

From there I go straight to, *This will never work. He has models coming on to him after his shows. He'll be forty-nine when you're turning sixty. He is young and hip, and you don't even know the hip word for* hip *anymore. You belong at home in bed with a book.*

I remind myself that this is what I always say and what I always do. As soon as I'm in a relationship, I promote fear from clerk to president, even though all it can do is sweep up, turn off the lights, and lock the door.

I am so deep in my own argument that I almost don't hear Seth say, "Sophie."

He stops me on the pavement and turns me toward him. His face practically glows white; he is a ghost of the ghost he usually looks like.

He says, "When did you go out with him?"

"So long ago he had a different name."

"Beelzebub?"

I tell him that Vincent was still in purgatory when I knew him.

"But it was hard for you to see him with somebody else, tonight?"

"No," I say, a little surprised.

He nods, not quite believing. "But the thing you said about her being a model?"

"Models are always hard," I say. "And it was hard to see her necking with your cheek."

After I've said this, I want to say that I don't usually use the word *neck* as a verb; it's a fifties word, my mother's word, but he is shaking his head and I can see he is not thinking about how old I sound or look or am.

"Obviously he still has a thing for you," Seth says, and shakes his head and swallows a couple of times, like he's trying to get rid of a bad taste. "The way he looked at you."

My *phew* gives me an Indian burn of shame. "That look was for Amanda's sake," I say, and I know it's true. For a second, I am an older sister to my younger self. "If she brings it up later, he'll tell her she's crazy."

"Very nice," Seth says, and his voice tells me that he doesn't want to hear any more about Vincent and Amanda, he doesn't care about them, and that he's wishing he didn't care so much about me.

It scares me. But then I get this big feeling, simple but exalted: *He's like me, just with different details.*

His eyes are closed, and I think maybe he's picturing me with Vincent or other men he assumes I've slept with or loved. Maybe he's telling himself that he's too tall or doesn't hear well enough.

Usually he pulls me in for the hug, but now I do it. I pull him in and we stay like this, his chin on my head, my face on his chest.

I find myself picturing Amanda at another party with Vincent and feeling sorry for her. It occurs to me that if I were as beautiful as she is, every passing half-birthday would be harder to celebrate. But mostly I am just glad I am not her and glad we are not them and glad just to be out here on the curb, breathing the sweet air of Williamsburg and postcolonial freedom.

We are quiet for a while, walking. I begin to see where we are now. We pass the Miss Williamsburg Diner. Little bookstores I could spend my life in. We pass a gallery with mobiles hung above a reflecting pool.

Then we're standing in a parking lot, outside of what Seth tells me is Bob's restaurant. I'm saying that living in Manhattan gives you a heightened appreciation of parking lots when Seth takes something out of his pocket and puts it in my hand. It's a dollar. "For the gift shop," he says. "Don't lose it now."

With my dollar hand, I squeeze Seth's about thirty-seven times, telling him everything I feel.

He says, "What does that mean?"

I say, " 'I'm hungry.' "

What I feel is, *Right now I am having the life I want, here outside the Shiny Diner, Bob's, or the Wonder Spot, with my dollar to spend and dinner to come.* We will try everything on the menu. Then we will drive through Brooklyn and cross the bridge with the Manhattan skyline in front of us, which looks new to me every time I see it, and we will drive right into it. We'll find a parking space a few blocks from my apartment on Tenth Street, and we'll pick up milk and tomorrow's paper. We will undress and get into bed.

FOR THE BEST IN PAPERBACKS, LOOK FOR THE (penguin)

In every corner of the world, on every subject under the sun, Penguin represents quality and variety—the very best in publishing today.

For complete information about books available from Penguin—including Penguin Classics, Penguin Compass, and Puffins—and how to order them, write to us at the appropriate address below. Please note that for copyright reasons the selection of books varies from country to country.

In the United States: Please write to *Penguin Group (USA), P.O. Box 12289 Dept. B, Newark, New Jersey 07101-5289* or call 1-800-788-6262.

In the United Kingdom: Please write to *Dept. EP, Penguin Books Ltd, Bath Road, Harmondsworth, West Drayton, Middlesex UB7 0DA.*

In Canada: Please write to *Penguin Books Canada Ltd, 90 Eglinton Avenue East, Suite 700, Toronto, Ontario M4P 2Y3.*

In Australia: Please write to *Penguin Books Australia Ltd, P.O. Box 257, Ringwood, Victoria 3134.*

In New Zealand: Please write to *Penguin Books (NZ) Ltd, Private Bag 102902, North Shore Mail Centre, Auckland 10.*

In India: Please write to *Penguin Books India Pvt Ltd, 11 Panchsheel Shopping Centre, Panchsheel Park, New Delhi 110 017.*

In the Netherlands: Please write to *Penguin Books Netherlands bv, Postbus 3507, NL-1001 AH Amsterdam.*

In Germany: Please write to *Penguin Books Deutschland GmbH, Metzlerstrasse 26, 60594 Frankfurt am Main.*

In Spain: Please write to *Penguin Books S. A., Bravo Murillo 19, 1° B, 28015 Madrid.*

In Italy: Please write to *Penguin Italia s.r.l., Via Benedetto Croce 2, 20094 Corsico, Milano.*

In France: Please write to *Penguin France, Le Carré Wilson, 62 rue Benjamin Baillaud, 31500 Toulouse.*

In Japan: Please write to *Penguin Books Japan Ltd, Kaneko Building, 2-3-25 Koraku, Bunkyo-Ku, Tokyo 112.*

In South Africa: Please write to *Penguin Books South Africa (Pty) Ltd, Private Bag X14, Parkview, 2122 Johannesburg.*